John Creasey – Master Storyteller

Born in Surrey, England in 1908 ir
were nine children, John Creasey g
teller and international sensation. F
and thriller titles have now sold 8C
These include many popular series
The Toff, *Dr Palfrey* and *The Baron*.

Creasy wrote under many pseudonyms, explaining that booksellers had complained he totally dominated the 'C' section in stores. They included:

> *Gordon Ashe, M E Cooke, Norman Deane, Robert Caine Frazer, Patrick Gill, Michael Halliday, Charles Hogarth, Brian Hope, Colin Hughes, Kyle Hunt, Abel Mann, Peter Manton, J J Marric, Richard Martin, Rodney Mattheson, Anthony Morton* and *Jeremy York*.

Never one to sit still, Creasey had a strong social conscience, and stood for Parliament several times, along with founding the One Party Alliance which promoted the idea of government by a coalition of the best minds from across the political spectrum.

He also founded the British Crime Writers' Association, which to this day celebrates outstanding crime writing. The Mystery Writers of America bestowed upon him the Edgar Award for best novel and then in 1969 the ultimate Grand Master Award. John Creasey's stories are as compelling today as ever.

The Toff Series

A Bundle for the Toff
A Doll for the Toff
A Knife for the Toff
A Mask for the Toff
A Rocket for the Toff
A Score for the Toff
Accuse the Toff
Break the Toff
Call the Toff
Double for the Toff
Feathers for the Toff
Follow the Toff
Fool the Toff
Hammer the Toff
Here Comes the Toff
Hunt the Toff
Introducing the Toff
Kill the Toff
Leave It to the Toff
Kiss the Toff
Model for the Toff
Poison for the Toff
Salute the Toff
Stars for the Toff
Terror for the Toff
The Kidnapped Child
The Toff among the Millions
The Toff and Old Harry
The Toff and the Crooked Copper
The Toff and the Deadly Parson
The Toff and the Deep Blue Sea
The Toff and the Fallen Angels
The Toff and the Golden Boy
The Toff and the Great Illusion
The Toff and the Lady
The Toff and the Runaway Bride
The Toff and the Sleepy Cowboy
The Toff and the Spider
The Toff and the Stolen Tresses
The Toff and the Toughs
The Toff and the Terrified Taxman
The Toff and the Trip-Trip-Triplets
The Toff at Butlins
The Toff at the Fair
The Toff Breaks In
The Toff Goes On
The Toff Goes to Market
The Toff in New York
The Toff in Town
The Toff in Wax
The Toff Is Back
The Toff on Board
The Toff on Fire
The Toff Proceeds
The Toff Steps Out
The Toff Takes Shares
Vote for the Toff

Murder Out of the Past (short stories)
The Toff on the Trail (short stories)

The Toff Breaks In

John Creasey

HOUSE OF STRATUS

This edition published in 2014 by House of Stratus, an imprint of
Stratus Books Ltd., Lisandra House, Fore Street,
Looe, Cornwall, PL13 1AD, U.K.
www.houseofstratus.com

Typeset by House of Stratus.

A catalogue record for this book is available from the British Library and the Library of Congress.

ISBN 07551-3660-8
EAN 978-07551-3660-5

Prologue

Partly 1910

The heat was terrific, scorching the skin of the two men who struggled across the parched desert of Central Australia – men whom the burning sun and the dry sand drove almost mad. It worked into their food, their water-bottles, their eyes and mouths and noses; they were never free of it. But they kept their sanity, for gold drove them on. The lure of gold, which they knew existed ten, twenty, perhaps thirty miles away. There was water, too, now almost as vital as the yellow dust.

Hour after hour passed, and slowly the sun moved across the brazen heavens, finally to sink below a line of distant mountains. There was no breeze, but the shades of night brought coolness.

One of the men spoke, his voice cracked and hoarse.

'Another two hours,' he muttered. 'No more than that, and we'll be through.'

There was an ugly scowl on the other's face.

'Unless Robertson's beaten us to it.'

'He can't—' began the first speaker; but he lapsed into silence without completing the sentence. It *was* just possible that another prospector could have reached that oasis of water and gold before them. If he had …

Slowly they went on until suddenly the desert was broken, and in the distance they saw shrubs and stunted trees. One of the men sniffed, and his eyes glittered. He broke into a run, stiff and pain-racked though he was, and there was a word croaking from his lips, a magic word in that barren desert.

'Water, thank God, water!'

'Quiet, you fool!' his companion snapped viciously. 'Look there—'

Both men stopped, for in the distance they could see the glow of a small fire, evidence of another man's presence. They *had* been beaten to that oasis of water and gold. There was water enough for them all, but the gold belonged to the first-comer.

Black hatred towards the unseen man possessed them.

Even more slowly they made their way towards the fire until gradually the man was visible, a silhouette against the uneven red glow. Both men were breathing hard, and their right hands were on the butts of guns – heavy Colts, for in 1910 the Colt .45 was a popular weapon.

'No,' muttered one man suddenly. 'We—we can't do it.'

His companion's voice was vicious.

'That claim is ours, we've got to have it after this and, by God, *he* won't stop me!'

They were near that solitary figure, within easy shooting distance, and still they had not been observed; the only sound was the cracking of burning wood and the hum of insects.

The first man drew his gun. A loud roar came as flame stabbed through the darkness, and by the fire the solitary prospector threw up his arms and collapsed. Through the quiet came moans mingling with curses, dwindling slowly to an incoherent muttering.

The others broke into a shambling run towards him. When they reached him he was lying still, flat on his face. They turned him over roughly.

'Look!' The gunman kneeling beside the corpse stared down at the dead face. 'It's not him! It's not Robertson! Robertson's not here yet ...'

They felt fear surging through them, panic on its heels. This was a stranger. Robertson, the only other man who knew of the gold at this spot, whom they had been racing across the desert, had not arrived.

But – they knew Robertson *would* come.

'He said that he'd bring others—he's sent one in advance.' The murderer brushed his hand across his lips. 'We ought to have known. They'll be here soon, and they'll find this. Find this!'

'Shut up!' The second man looked round, seeing that the lonely traveller had provisions in plenty; Robertson probably had sent this man to guard the gold-claim. No one could have crossed that stretch of desert alone with the big load of provisions and trappings which the dead man had near by. Others were probably close at hand.

'We'll have to go,' he said. 'We'll take his food, make up-country for a few miles, and then rest for the night. We can push on tomorrow.'

Within an hour they were on their way, with fear instead of avarice to drive them and goad them. It drove them temporarily to safety although with little time to spare – but most important it drove them into intrigue and crime that was to be with them all their lives.

They did not know that then.

Nor did they realise that it had taken them irrevocably into the orbit of the Hon. Richard Rollison, who at that time was preparing without trepidation – nerves were never to be a characteristic of his – for his first departure from the wings of his parents to the ministrations of schoolmasters. Which masters quickly came to the conclusion that if Rollison wanted to do a thing it would be done, regardless of the consequences. Some even prophesied for him a sticky end.

The Toff – as Rollison came to be known – was the last to dwell on his days at Charterhouse and Cambridge, where he gained fame and his cricket blue, and by some remarkable means avoided a battle with the dons. He had a way with him, had Rollison, against which the sternest proctor wilted, but probably the reason he avoided the indignity of being sent down was his habit of doing misdeeds mostly on his own.

Some said that Cambridge began his quite abnormal dislike of certain types of crime. Others claimed that he had been born amoral in some things, but oddly righteous in others. Still more decided that it was the unreasonable fortune which a misguided grandfather left him that enabled him to encourage his own peculiar tastes.

England had not been large enough to hold him.

A year out of Cambridge, with a first in Classics which had surprised everyone but his tutors, he began a five-year tour of the world – and not by luxury liner. The holds of cargo-boats and small tramps had a great deal to do with the development of his bone, muscle, experience and first-hand knowledge of the most unlikely crimes and their exponents. There was, for instance, the tramp plying from London to the Barbary Coast and manned by three murderers, two white-slavers, a God-fearing skipper and a Devil-defying first-mate who liked rum more than his own soul. With the discovery that there was gold in the hold a mutiny not only threatened, but took place – and the Toff and cabin-boy guided the ship into port, with the crew in irons and the skipper in his bunk.

In the course of his travels by sea and land the Toff learned to differentiate between crime and crime. On his black-list were blackmail, murder, robbery with violence, drug-trafficking and white-slavery, and later he learned to dislike company frauds and most confidence tricksters with similar intensity, although no one who outwitted a millionaire gave him much concern.

In those five years of travelling, too, the Toff earned the first rumours of his reputation.

He was a handsome man, and darkly tanned; he had grey eyes that could smile one moment and be very cold the next, he was tall and lithe and yet muscular. Remarkable stories circulated about him, although at first he had no idea of them. In his remarkable way he was happy …

But he possessed an orderly mind.

His life was too haphazard, and his dislike of crime – especially the items on his black-list – increased. He began to look for examples of it, and to pick out the perpetrators for his special brand of retribution, not always in accordance with the law. Twice, in fact, he was frowned upon by the authorities in Shanghai and Chicago, and politely but firmly requested to leave the localities – which he did, being tired of them and saying so in a way which did not cause offence until he was out of earshot. Whispers of his activities grew apace; the number of people with reason to hate him also grew. From Chicago to Stamboul, San Francisco to Marseilles, Shanghai to Paris, the whispers travelled. It was said that he carried death in his two fists, that he could shoot and throw a knife with equal accuracy, that his smile and his laughter were of the Devil, that he could be in two places at once, and that he had never been known to fail to get his man.

And so the Toff reached London, preceded by his reputation.

Within a year he was more feared in certain circles than any man – or organization – in London, including Scotland Yard. He worked mostly on his own, although a certain Chief-Inspector Horace McNab had good reasons to bless and to curse him in turn.

His chief weapon was fear – the other man's fear – and he called it psychological terrorism. Out of the blue he would drop on his victim, his grey eyes sparkling, his shapely lips curving, his voice filled with all the mockery in the world. And then he would strike – and soon afterwards the gates of one of His Majesty's rest homes for the crooked in mind were opened to admit another unwilling guest. But the name of the Toff rarely figured in the official records of the case. Usually Chief Inspector McNab took the kudos, and was duly grateful until such time as the Toff snatched a small-time crook out of his grasp. For the Toff loved some small rogues, and helped them when he could.

Despite the misguided conception of some people, of the type rigidly superstitious, the Toff was not omniscient. True, he heard rumours of many crimes so that he could stop them before they materialised, but that was because so many people who haled Scotland Yard looked on the Toff as their guardian angel. They learned that if they asked him to say nothing to the police, nothing was said. He was at once the most-hated and the best-loved man in that place euphemistically called the Underworld, and he became almost a legend, which was what he wanted.

To help the legend, he prepared a number of visiting cards with his name and address on one side, and on the other the pencilled drawing of a top hat, a monocle and a cigarette, and a face that wasn't there. That, of course, was after he had been dubbed the Toff by a little East Ender with an appreciation of good tailoring. He had innumerable agents, and learned many incredible things, but some escaped him. For instance, the habits and practices of a Mr. Arnold Chamberlain, which even the Toff would have admitted was no name for a villain.

But it was due, if unwittingly, to Mr. Chamberlain that he heard so many years afterwards of a murder which had been committed in Australia's Central Desert; and into his hand fell the axe of retribution.

Chapter One

Mr. Augustus Meer

Mr. Augustus Meer, tall, frail and grey-haired, had a pair of benevolent weak blue eyes that surveyed the quiet world around him through horn-rimmed – and some said rose-coloured – spectacles. It was as though he found not a single thing to displease him, and if he read the scare-heads of the daily papers during the recurring crisis that threatened to put the world in chaos, he did not say so. No one thought of asking Mr. Meer what he thought of Mr. Malenkov, for instance; it was so obvious that he would harbour only kindly sentiments, and in times of crises kindly sentiments were not seriously wanted.

In the old-world but A.R.P. infested town of Hersham, in Sussex, Mr. Meer was respected and popular, and looked on with warm if sometimes slightly tolerant esteem. Children especially liked him. He was like a godfather spreading kindly arms over the sick and the poor.

He was also a dealer in antiques, a dabbler in philately – he never called it stamp-collecting – and a connoisseur of wines. His friends were legion. During the days when he was well enough to attend his little shop in the High Street he would talk to every client not as a salesman but as a glowing fellow-enthusiast. Experts from all over England visited Mr. Meer and were startled by the value of many of his pieces. And yet, despite the excellence of his trade and the genuineness of his antiques, Mr. Meer's bank balance was not large.

Twice in a year he was forced to ask a friend and next-door neighbour, Simonson, of the London-National Bank, to oblige him with a small overdraft.

'My dear fellow,' said Simonson, a jovial-faced if worldly man, on the second occasion, 'it's a pleasure to help you, but—and I know you won't take this badly—you really shouldn't give so much money to charity. It's—'

'Provided I have enough to eat and drink,' said Augustus Meer in his curiously mellow voice, 'and friends like yourself, I have nothing to worry about. If I can make the lot of less fortunate people better, I am satisfied.'

Simonson was touched in more ways than one.

Another man in Hersham, Dr. Vincent Lowerby, uttered a different warning with more vehemence.

'You must take things more heartily, Meer; you're a healthy man, even if you think you're not. You can't be more than fifty-five, yet I've heard that you spend two or three whole days a week in bed. It's unhealthy, I tell you; you'll rue it later.'

Mr. Augustus Meer shrugged his shoulders.

'I get so fatigued,' he said. 'But you must not concern yourself, my dear doctor. My trouble is more—er—inertia, shall we say?—than anything else.'

'I know all about that,' said Vincent Lowerby, a tall, aggressively hearty man of middle age. 'But you're rusting away down here.'

'I'm very happy,' said Meer softly; yet there was a far from soft expression in his eyes which a more observant man than Dr. Lowerby would have noticed.

The doctor, however, was concerned with more important things. He lacked scruple; and he had discovered that he could pick up antiques from Augustus Meer at ridiculously low prices, and dispose of them to a certain Mr. Arnold Chamberlain, of London, at two hundred per cent profit or more.

That day the doctor purchased a Chippendale cabinet, slightly damaged, wished Mr. Meer good-bye and reiterated his advice, and delivered the cabinet a few hours later to Arnold Chamberlain's Oxford Street salerooms.

Chamberlain was out, but Lowerby was not worried, for he knew that he would get his money. Also he knew, or thought he did, a lot of things about Mr. Arnold Chamberlain. In the first place he had learned that the man was a fur-importer with warehouses in Wapping and salerooms in Oxford Street. He posed as an American business man, and he certainly looked and acted the part.

What Dr. Vincent Lowerby realised besides these ordinary facts, however, was that Chamberlain trafficked in dope and stolen jewels. Lowerby knew that for a very good reason: he helped Arnold Chamberlain in his illegal traffic. It was not difficult, however, for Lowerby to explain if necessary the presence of certain drugs, although he – on Chamberlain's advice and with details supplied by the fur-importer – handled them with great care, and was not suspected by the local police.

From Chamberlain's showrooms, and with the cheque as good as in his pocket, Lowerby went to a block of mansion-flats hi Piccadilly, where he was amused by a lady whose charms the Toff would not have considered pleasing. It was an odd but inescapable fact that the Toff – as the Hon. Richard Rollison – was walking past the mansion-flats as Lowerby went in. The Toff, who was with an Austrian film star of world-acknowledged charm, saw and noticed, as was his way, that the man who entered the mansions was large and red-faced.

It was some time before he saw Lowerby again.

It was also to be some time before he saw the film star, who was wanted in Hollywood. Persuading her that he would be desolated was a full-time task even for Rollison, but he contrived it, and bade her good-bye, and told himself that he would like a different kind of amusement. This he confided to Jolly, who was his man.

Jolly's appearance was impeccable, but not in accordance with his name. Not only did he always dress in black, but usually he looked on the verge of tears. Some said it was indigestion, but the Toff knew that it was simply Jolly's way.

As the Toff entered his Gresham Terrace flat, Jolly was dusting with care a remarkable collection of knives, pistols, daggers, cartridges, weapons old, young and middle-aged, which adorned one of the walls of the lounge. The Toff, in his wilder moments, would claim that each and every weapon had at one time been used to try to end his life, but that was an exaggeration; he had, however, collected them during his varied exploits, and between he and Jolly was wagered a constant battle as to what would fittingly go on the wall. The larger pieces Jolly kept in a box-room museum.

'Good afternoon, sir,' said Jolly. 'Tea, sir?'

'I suppose so,' said the Toff.

'Perhaps with a little lacing of rum, sir?'

'Where did you get that pagan idea?' demanded the Toff. 'I will drink tea, and if it's really necessary I'll drink rum, but I will not have lacings, and I've told you so before. Jolly, I have an urge to action.'

'I am not surprised, sir,' said Jolly.

'Any post?' asked the Toff.

'At your elbow, sir.'

The Toff saw three bills and a typewritten letter. Opening this, he frowned.

The Ridings,
Hersham,
Sussex.

Dear Rollison,

Forgive this hurried and last-minute note. Expecting you to be busy with the County for the summer, I did not include you in the invitations for my Annual Cricket Week here, but seeing that you seem to be playing only occasionally, it occurs to me that you can slip down for some of the games. Good ones, I assure you – Cozens among others will be down.

Do try to come. The opening match is on Monday – three days ahead – so there is good time to let me know.

Sincerely,
George Mannering.

To Rollison cricket was more than a pastime; it was a minor religion. The ground at the Ridings was of county class, and although he was due to play for Midshire the following week, he doubted whether a sprained tendon would stand up to three days hard. Two or three amiable country-house matches would enable him to loosen up thoroughly for bigger games, and to test the tendon.

Mannering, he knew, was the Chief Constable of Sussex, an affable gentleman who had two main objects in life – cricket and the effective control of his Constabulary. The Ridings was a dream-place, an Elizabethan Manor little spoiled by modernization.

Jolly brought tea.

'Jolly,' said the Toff, 'I am going to Sir George Mannering's for a few days; pack enough for a week.'

'Immediately, sir?'

'I start in the morning.'

'Your gear goes with you, sir?'

'It does; and don't soak that new bat in linseed oil,' directed the Toff.

He telephoned Mannering, who sounded delighted, and talked for ten minutes. Thereafter the Toff bathed, and later dined alone, read a futurist novel with some enjoyment and no little cynicism, and retired early.

He did not know that a Mr. Sanderson and his daughter, on the advice of Arnold Chamberlain, were planning to visit the Hersham district early in the following week —but were not anticipating sudden death.

Chamberlain had found little difficulty in interesting James Sanderson, without telling the latter just why. It was after he had done so that he went to the Oxford Street salerooms – some hours after Mr. Meer had retired to his bed. He saw the cabinet that Vincent Lowerby had delivered, and rubbed his hands.

He sat in front of it, manipulated a drawer, and after a moment took out a small wash-leather bag. From the bag he took a little heap of precious stones: diamonds, rubies, emeralds and sapphires, all scintillating in the brilliant electric light. He ran them through his hands for some seconds, smiling, but not pleasantly.

'I wonder what you would say if you knew just what you bring me,' he said aloud, and he was thinking of Lowerby. 'However, you know enough. A little more and you would be dangerous.'

He laughed, and ran the jewels through his fingers again before locking them in a wall-safe. Then he drew a cheque for Dr. Vincent Lowerby, in excessive payment for the Chippendale cabinet, sealed the envelope, and rang a bell with the push on his desk. To the grinning negro who responded he said: 'All prepared for tomorrow, the two of you?'

'Yes, bo'.'

'All right, don't make any mistakes, and get it over quickly. You can clear off for the night now, and post this on the way.'

He tossed Lowerby's letter to the negro, who caught it neatly, grinned, and stalked out. Ten minutes later two men slipped from the back of the premises, the negro and a tall, thin, bearded Chinaman; a queer combination, and one which would have interested the Toff greatly.

Chapter Two

Visitors To Sussex

On the Monday, which was the day when Rollison was to play for Sir George Mannering's XI against a strong team of South of England amateurs, James Sanderson finished putting his tie on, a task which twenty-five years of practice had never perfected in him, when his bedroom door opened abruptly and his daughter entered.

'*Aren't* you ready yet, darling?'

Sanderson smiled.

'Kept you waiting again, have I? Don't let it worry you, Syl; when you get a husband you can train him better. I'm nearly through, and—*what's* the matter now?'

'You can't go out in that tie,' said Sylvia firmly.

'By heck I can—and will.'

But he doubted it. Sylvia rummaged through a drawer and selected one of a soberer hue, and stood by him while he slipped it inside his collar, after taking the first one off. He topped her by six inches, a tall, broad-shouldered, clean-looking man of middle age, with something of the rancher, the man of wide spaces, in his loose-limbed body and far-seeing grey eyes. His voice was the kind to be heard often on the Australian plains.

He was reflecting, as she tied his knot, that he let her have her own way too much. Bound to happen, perhaps, when there was no one else to help to control her. Not that she had needed much controlling; she had the sound common sense that his daughter should have had, and was capable enough, even if the heiress to his considerable fortune. Nothing sheltered or secluded about her life! She could sit a horse with any man, and take her part in any conversation, any company.

'That's better,' she said. 'And now don't dare to tell me you haven't had breakfast.'

'Before you were awake,' smiled Sanderson. 'I've been out for a walk, Syl.'

'So *that's* why you're late. Dad, you're impossible at times; you know I'm dying to get down to this place, and yet you fiddle and waste time, and—'

'Turn round,' said Sanderson, and he swung her round easily and spanked her with his free hand. 'Get your hat, if you're going to wear one.'

Sanderson waited for her in the foyer of the hotel.

When she did come she wore an absurdly small hat on the waves of her dark hair, with a tailor-made suit that discreetly emphasised a figure no man would complain about. Her hands and feet were tiny, the latter neatly shod, and the smile on well-shaped lips was matched by the gleam in her grey eyes. Most people would have said that she looked happy as she walked by her father's side to the Rolls-Royce which was standing outside the doors of the hotel in Piccadilly.

'Driving yourself?' she asked.

'Yes, we'll see this on our own.'

'That's grand,' said Sylvia. 'Ye old Manor House for new-rich cousins from Australia. If we go there, Dad, the country folk will probably turn their long noses up at us.'

'It depends on how you behave,' said Sanderson, 'and' – he chuckled – 'how many young bloods there are who aren't married or engaged.'

'If you think a mere engagement will put me off ...' Sylvia laughed. 'You are a fool, aren't you? But, Dad, the place does sound just right, doesn't it? What agent sent you the particulars?'

'None,' said Sanderson.

'Now what exactly do you mean?'

He was driving through the thick traffic near Hyde Park Corner. The girl imagined that his expression had altered, but it might have been the concentration on his driving. Yet she had seen that frown too often of late – as if he were worried by something he would not discuss.

He spoke abruptly.

'Chamberlain put me on to it, Syl.'

'Oh.' The smile disappeared from her eyes. 'I don't like that man at all.'

'I know you don't.'

'And why should he have gone to that trouble—you only bought a small fur cape from him, and—'

'If you call a hundred guineas small, I don't,' said Sanderson, smiling again. 'You jump to likes and dislikes too quickly, you know; you always have done.'

'I know when a man can be trusted, and Chamberlain can't,' said Sylvia shortly. 'And I can't understand why you took to him, either.'

'It wasn't a case of taking to him. He sold me the cape, and we got talking—he knew about the house. If it's as good as it sounds, we won't worry who introduced it to us.'

Sylvia was silent until they got out of London and on to the Hersham road. By then the June sun, the green countryside so unlike that at 'home', the wooded patches on either side of the road and the absence of those long, monotonous stretches of scrub, made her forget her dislike of Arnold Chamberlain, forget that from time to time she had felt that her father was worried.

It was good to be in England, and this part seemed as pleasing as any she had seen. If the details of the house they were going to inspect were accurate, it was an Elizabethan gem in the heights near Hersham, standing in two hundred acres, mostly of parkland.

Sanderson drove fast. In under two hours they reached Hersham and examined the directions Chamberlain had given. Out on the Brighton road, the third turning left, and then a signpost would direct him to Wyndham Manor. He followed the details and ten minutes afterwards climbed out of the Rolls to open the wrought-iron gates of Chamberlain's recommended residence.

The first impression was good.

The parkland had not been neglected, and at that time of the year was at its best. As they drove along the macadam drive a dozen rabbits scurried from a patch of grass into the tangled undergrowth of bramble and young fern. Giant chestnut trees and mighty oaks were unfurling their leaves to greet the sky; the blueness of the sky had a hard, metallic loveliness heralding heat.

Sylvia exclaimed suddenly.

'Oh, look!'

The house justified the exclamation.

It was built half-way along a gradual slope, grass- and tree-clad except for half an acre or more about the house itself, where lawns, although not lately mown, had not yet grown long, and a small rose-walk was already rioting in colour. Gabled and oak-beamed, the house was neither large nor small, but with its mullioned windows and old brickwork it looked superb.

'Like it?' Sanderson smiled.

'*Like* it! It's just perfect, Jimmy; it couldn't be better! No, don't let's go in first, we'll drive up as far as we can and then walk round—it's more fun.'

'All right,' agreed Sanderson.

It was twenty minutes before he unlocked the front door with a key Chamberlain had supplied, and they stepped into a spacious oak-panelled hall, with parquet flooring. A staircase wide enough to be imposing faced them.

Sylvia lost herself in enthusiasm.

Sanderson's enjoyment was derived as much from her as from the house, although by the time they had finished the ground floor he had made up his mind that it was what he was looking for.

'We'd better go upstairs,' he said, 'and then find somewhere to eat, Syl. If you want to you can come back here for an hour or two this afternoon. I suppose,' he chuckled, 'if you learned Chamberlain was all kinds of a rogue, you wouldn't let it put you off this place?'

'You bet I wouldn't,' said Sylvia downrightly. 'Don't dawdle so, I want to see the bedrooms. And' – she stopped suddenly. 'I suppose there are bathrooms?'

'Three, I'm told.'

'I'd take it with one, *and* an old-fashioned bath,' said Sylvia. She ran up the stairs lightly, ahead of her father, and at the top she stopped. He saw her stare towards the end of the wide landing, and as he reached her she said with a forced lightness: 'It was the echo, I suppose; I thought I heard a sound.'

'Could be a tramp making free of the place,' said Sanderson.

He smiled lo himself when he saw that she did not go ahead of him again, but she was soon filled with further enthusiasm for the upstairs rooms. From all windows views of the sweeping downland presented themselves, green and delightful in the sun. From the south rooms it was possible to see the spire of Hersham church, but no other house or habitation was visible.

'Next floor?' said Sanderson.

'Yes, of course, we want to see it all.' She let him go to the stairs first, and held his arm as they went up. 'You didn't hear anything, did you?'

'Nothing but mice,' said Sanderson. 'I—'

He broke off.

Sylvia's hand tightened about his arm as she saw the man who came from a room directly ahead of them. Any man would have made her jump, but the negro who stood there, unsmiling and monstrous, unnerved her. She stepped back a pace without relinquishing her grip on Sanderson's arm, and she felt the sudden tensing of his muscles.

'Dad—what—'

'Get away,' snapped Sanderson. 'Get away fast; don't—'

'Not so easy, *Mister* Sanderson.' A voice came from immediately behind them, and Sylvia swung round—to find a tall, bearded Chinaman, dressed in European clothes, eyeing her without expression. His English was perfect, except for a slight slurring of the vowels.

Sanderson snapped: 'If you two—'

It happened very quickly.

She heard the negro say, 'We've found yuh, okay!' and she saw the vicious grin on his face. The Chinaman's hands tightened on her shoulders, and she was forced away from her father, Sanderson dropped his right hand to his pocket; she saw him try to draw out a gun, glimpsed the grey steel. But the negro moved too quickly for him, crashed a vast fist into his stomach. Sanderson gasped as he doubled up.

And then Sylvia saw the knife.

It flashed downwards from the negro's hand as Sanderson tried to get away. It struck, and she screamed – but no sound came, for a yellow hand tightened about her throat. Standing, staring, terror within her, she saw the stroke which cut into her father's throat.

She saw the blood.

She collapsed, consciousness leaving her, and the Chinaman stopped her from falling. He carried her with little effort down the stairs, and at the bottom secured her wrists and ankles thoroughly before returning to the second landing and helping the negro to move the body of the man Chamberlain had introduced to Wyndham Manor.

The girl remained unconscious while the Chinaman drove the Rolls, and the negro a smaller car, which followed. They went for a while through the lovely countryside and the burning sun, and among the places they passed was the cricket field of the Ridings. White-flannelled figures were dotted on it, among them that of the Hon. Richard Rollison, who was enjoying himself, with no thought of crime in his mind.

No thought of murder.

Nor did that change during the day, or the night when, after their fill of beer and Sir George's overloaded table, the guests and visiting team played billiards, or talked, or made a poker-school, and generally felt the well-being that the Toff believed an integral part of a game of cricket, and at least half of its attraction.

A cyclist free-wheeling down the hill leading into Hersham saw a clear stretch of road in front of him and drank in the beauty of the Downlands that stretched on all sides. It was peaceful and quiet, and it was pleasant not to have to push.

And then, as he passed a disused quarry near the road, he saw something huddled at the bottom; at that moment a shaft of sunlight lit upon it.

The cyclist stopped and looked down. There was a sudden alarm in him, for the huddled thing was ominously still, yet like a man.

It *was* the body of a man, dressed like a tramp, and at the neck a wicked cut.

The cyclist leapt on his bike and rushed into Hersham, no longer free-wheeling or enjoying the scene. At the police-station he gasped out news of his discovery; and twenty minutes later he was sitting next to the driver of a police car, agitatedly describing the exact spot where he had seen the body.

But when he reached the spot again the body was not there!

Some blood was; but the local inspector, a dubious man where talk of death by violence was concerned, doubted little but that the cyclist – a local youth – had killed a rabbit and hoped to create a sensation; he knew that such things happened. But he was cautious and said little, for which he was glad; for a few hours later the nearest doctor had examined and tested the blood, to declare it human.

So much blood had drained into the turf that it seemed that the missing victim of the puzzling affair must have bled to death, even if the wound in his throat had not been fatal at the moment of incision. The cyclist was vindicated, the inspector perturbed enough to go at once to the Chief Constable and report – a daring thing on the day of a cricket match.

'From the time this cyclist—a lad named Meakings—saw the body,' said burly Inspector Dawbury, 'to the time we arrived at the quarry, less than three-quarters of an hour passed, Sir George. That means—'

'That at least two men went down into the quarry and pulled the body up to the road,' said Sir George Mannering, a big, blond, typical country-gentleman. 'Was there any sign of blood leading from the patch at the bottom, Dawbury?'

'None at all,' said Dawbury.

'Well, get a message through to London. We'll want an SOS sent out so that we can get hold of any motorist who passed the quarry at whatever time Meakings did. When was that?'

'Five past ten, sir, as near as I can say.'

'Then say between ten o'clock and eleven. See to that, will you, without losing time. And you'll want a search party on the go at once.'

'Of course, sir. Will you be asking Scotland Yard for assistance?'

'No,' said Mannering testily. 'We only want the general call; we can handle the rest. If anything develops, let me know at once.'

Dawbury saluted and left the Chief Constable, who was dressed in white flannels spoiled by a green patch on one knee, glancing impatiently at the clock. It was five past one. 'Almost time for lunch,' Mannering said aloud. 'Blast this business; it would happen this week. If nothing's turned up I'll have to get busy myself.'

The clock in the library was fast, as it happened, and Mannering strolled towards the field as the last over was being called. A tall, lean player was at the batting-crease, and his sunburned face showed a smile which even at that distance revealed his white teeth. He lifted his bat waist-high, put his left foot forward, and came down hard on a fast ball, pitched well up. The leather flew along the grass, making a thin red line and rattling against the wooden walls of the pavilion. There was a little burst of hand-clapping, and the batsman waved his hand, still smiling and with reason happy. The yokel manipulating the scoring-board put the figure 50 opposite batsman number 3.

A little wizened man in spotless flannels strolled towards the Chief Constable. That was Cozens, hero of a hundred amateur centuries, a wizard with the bat and a man who had taken his toll off the best bowlers in England.

'Rollison's good,' said Cozens, watching the half-century-maker turn a short bumping ball safely past square leg. 'That cover drive of his—'

'I like his late cut best,' said Mannering. 'So few people use it these days.'

'He scores fast,' said Cozens, 'but he's got a defence like a brick wall. I'd like to see him against the South Africans this year.'

'D'you think he's got any chance?' asked Mannering.

'All the chance in the world—if he'd play more first-class cricket. But I fancy it ties him down too much.'

'Oh, does it?' muttered the Chief Constable, suddenly thoughtful. He was still looking preoccupied when, during the luncheon interval, he intercepted Rollison.

'Fine knock, Rolly,' said Mannering. 'It was good to watch.'

'I've been missed twice,' smiled Rollison. And then he saw the frown on his host's face, and added: 'Nothing disturbing the week, is there, Mannering?'

'Lord, do I show it as much as that? I'm not sure, yet. Are you busy? In that—er—unofficial business of yours, I mean; I know you never do any work.'

'Which is unkind, seeing how I've perspired to help your total,' retorted the Toff. 'No, I'm resting!'

'Will a little problem interest you?'

'Not if someone's lost a wallet.'

'This is serious. Look here, bring some sandwiches and a bottle of beer into my study, we'll have a chat then. If you don't mind,' added Sir George, quick to realise that mere murder must not over-ride his hospitality as a host.

'I've a feeling I'm going to like it,' said the Toff.

He heard the story as he ate sandwiches and drank beer, which at all times except cricketing times he abominated, or claimed to. Mannering made it dramatic, in parts, but the Toff showed neither surprise nor concern. Nor did he ask whether the cyclist had been drunk, but: 'Could it have been a hit-and-run accident?'

'I don't think so.'

'Hmmm. I'd like a word with the cyclist, if it could be done without hurting the excellent Dawbury's feelings.'

'Oh, nonsense! Dawbury'll do what I tell him. I'll arrange it, Rollison. Very good of you. Hope it doesn't spoil your game.'

'Spoil it?' smiled the Toff. 'It won't do that. You've asked for passing motorists, of course?'

'Oh, naturally.'

Rollison wondered how far he could trespass without putting Mannering's back up. 'I wonder if any of our fellows passed about then? Between ten and eleven would be their time, wouldn't it? The visiting team, I mean.'

Mannering stared.

'Good Gad, and I thought I'd covered everything! Thanks, Rollison. I—hmm! Not a subject I like introducing, you know. Think it would be all right if I ask for anyone who saw anything unusual?'

Again Rollison was puzzled.

Mannering was a good *C.C.* and self-reliant. Now he was virtually deferring to the Toff's judgment, and that was not by any means typical.

'I'd let 'em have the lot, I think; if they'd seen a body with the throat cut they'd have talked all right by now. Unless,' he added with apparent casualness, 'you think we're harbouring a throat-cutter in our sylvan midst.'

'God, no!' Mannering sheered from the suggestion, and whatever had prompted him to defer to the Toff was not the possibility that someone at the Ridings knew more than he should about the body. 'But I would like some action! I don't want the Yard fiddling about, and once this gets into the Press they'll be asking questions.'

'Well, let's get ours in first,' said the Toff.

He finished his sandwiches, smiling to himself at the transparency of bluff in Sir George Mannering. Mannering did not want the Yard consulted officially, but needed quick action: a body that was not a body and a murder that was only a might-be made him feel that someone else's judgment could be advisable – and there was the Toff, at hand.

The dining-room was a scene of some laughter, much talk, and many empty bottles. Not without regret the Toff regarded the still-loaded table and the many things he had missed. He began to feel a strong resentment against the man who had removed the body.

Mannering had a way with him. Two or three words had the attention of everyone present, and the blunt statement of facts caused a stir among some thirty men.

'The thing is,' said Mannering, 'that we know most of you passed the spot, and if anything unusual was seen it might be a help.'

There was a short silence, a murmur of conversation in asides, and considerable owlish concentration. Cricket, thought the Toff regretfully, did not necessarily breed an acute intelligence. A wizard with a ball with the shine knocked off could be a positive wallflower in a drawing-room. In quick succession five gentlemen assured Mannering that they hadn't seen a thing.

'Let's hear from those who did,' suggested the Toff.

Two men volunteered that they had passed the quarry about half past ten, when an Austin 20 saloon had been pulled up at the side of the road.

'Now I come to think of it,' said Bill Holding, a big, jovial-looking man who could make the ball turn both ways, 'there were a couple of fellows hauling a sack of something up. Turnips, I thought, or cabbages.'

'What were they like?' asked Rollison.

Holding rubbed his massive chin and concentrated.

'Well, I passed 'em pretty fast, old boy. One bloke had a beard; at least I think he did.'

'The other was a darkie,' broke in Tim Carteret, who had driven down at the same time. 'I was a few hundred yards behind Bill, and the couple had reached the top of the quarry. I saw the darkie's face, I mean. I wouldn't imagine it, would I?'

'Seeing you'll probably have to swear to it, I'd make sure,' said Rollison dryly. 'A negro, or just dark?'

'Pure negro, I'd say,' said Carteret. 'Coal-black—you know the kind. Damn' good fellows, some of them. I remember when the West Indians—'

'Did you see the man with the beard?' asked Rollison, quickly enough to make Carteret forget about the West Indies touring side.

'Oh, yes. A youngish, yellow-looking cove, in spite of the fungus.'

'Let's call the game a draw and make it a murder-hunt,' suggested a tall, wiry man who looked perpetually tired. 'It's damned hot already, and Rollison's sure to make us sweat this afternoon.'

The Toff appropriated a tomato.

'You leave murders to the police, Tommy,' he said; 'amateurs only bungle the job—ask Sir George. A word in your ear, Mannering ...'

Five minutes later he was putting a call through to Scotland Yard, and Mannering was saying that he did not like it. But he was forced to admit that the Austin 20 could have passed through a dozen counties between 10.30 a.m. and 1.30 p.m., it was not a matter for the Sussex police exclusively, and since the Yard's formal assistance had already been asked in this respect, there was little he could do about it.

Thus it was that Chief Inspector McNab heard of the mysterious affair in the quarry, and learned that the body had – presumably – been taken away by a negro and a man – perhaps yellow-skinned, with a beard – in an Austin car. Also that the Toff would be seeing him – McNab – some time, and meanwhile he hoped he was well.

Eleven weary fieldsmen, chasing the leather over the Ridings ground, wished that the Toff had taken the afternoon off. There was something in the peculiar affair of the morning which appeared to have sharpened his appetite for runs. He satisfied it by taking another hundred and seventeen off the perspiring visitors after lunch in something under seventy minutes, and then made a hash of an off-drive to give cover an easy catch.

'It's good to see you can make mistakes,' Carteret said as he congratulated him. 'Don't get the wrong man on the missing body, Rollison!'

'Want any help?' called Holding.

'Someone's been talking,' smiled Rollison.

He changed quickly, excused himself for dinner, and started for London soon after seven o'clock, thinking little about a drawn game. He wanted to find whether there was knowledge of a negro and a bearded man working together – a bearded man who, one of the members of the house-party had suggested, had looked Chinese. A combination which should be noticeable.

He did not intend to say too much to McNab, for he owed something to Mannering: but locating the negro and his companion was essential. A body with the throat cut, and then disappearing, had a touch of the bizarre that worried him. He felt rather than knew that this thing would go deep, unless it was stopped very quickly.

It was not stopped as quickly as he.

Five miles away from the Ridings a policeman came wobbling towards him on his cycle, with a hand outstretched.

'Mr. Rollison, sir?'

'That's right.'

'I just had a phone message, sir. Sir George Mannering wants you to call him, sir—there's a police-box just down the road; here's the key.'

He drove on thoughtfully.

Mannering was at the Ridings, and answered the call himself.

'Who is … oh, Rollison, I'm glad I caught you. Will you go straight to the quarry—where the body was seen, you know it—at once? I'll meet you there.'

'Clues at the scene?' demanded the Toff.

'No,' said Mannering, 'not necessarily. The body's back.'

Chapter Three

Puzzle For The Toff

The Toff replaced the receiver and pushed his hand through his dark hair. It was not his habit to admit a shock, but Mannering's cryptic statement had contrived one. He stepped from the blue police-box almost into the arms of the perspiring constable, who hoped he had got through all right.

'Yes, thanks,' said Rollison. 'Good night, officer. I—oh, a moment. How long have you been on duty?'

'Since nine this mornin', sir.'

'On this road all the time?'

'On an' off, sir, in a way of speaking. I goes round—'

'Where were you about half past ten?'

'Well, now, let me *see.*' Taking the interrogation as permission to remove his helmet and wipe a beaded forehead, the constable concentrated and, after several mis-hits, came to the conclusion that he had been on the main road between 10.15 and 10.45. Not exactly watching for bad drivers, he explained, but just keeping an eye open. Well, he couldn't remember *every* car that passed, but he did remember a black man driving a small one – too big for it, he seemed.

'Nice work,' said Rollison, 'that might prove very useful. I'll see that Sir George hears that you've got a memory.' He slipped his hand into his pocket. 'Was the car entirely on its own?'

The constable looked as if Rollison was asking whether it had had pups.

'Yessir—oh, you mean a trailer; no, sir, no trailer.'

'Ah,' said the Toff, and repressed his impatience. 'Was there another car in sight when it passed?'

'Now you're *askin'*,' said the constable with reproach. 'Maybe there was, an' maybe there wasn't. What kind of car would you be thinkin' of?'

'Largish. Like a big Austin. The driver might have been—'

'Got it! ' cried the constable in triumph. 'Funny little man with a beard. I remember because he looked a furriner and there was two furriners going close to each other, if you see what I mean. I wonder why I never remembered before? I —'

'Don't forget it now,' urged the Toff.

He rewarded the man with a half-crown and revved the engine to drown – quite accidentally – a startled thanks. The constable was still wondering if it was a tip or attempted bribery when Rollison reached the quarry, to find Mannering's car, with a small Morris nearby, already there. Three men were bending over something which they hid by their posterior bulk. Two uniformed men were standing nearby, and as Rollison slowed down, a police car with men carrying flashlight and finger-print apparatus arrived.

He approached the trio.

The ragged clothes of a man who was in a huddled heap beyond them suggested a tramp, thought Rollison, who went so quietly that he was nearly on top of the trio before Mannering heard him. The C.C. turned sharply, and then his face cleared.

'Oh, Rolly. I'm glad you've made it. Well—here it is.'

He motioned downwards, and the Toff regarded the huddled body, and the terrified face, of the dead man.

There was no doubting the manner of his death.

The phrase 'from ear to ear' was amply justified, but the crescent round his throat was no longer crimson, but a dirty brown, where the blood had coagulated. His face was unshaven, and twisted in sheer horror – here was a man who had looked death in the face and had not liked it. Yet he could not have lived a second after the first incision, and only a terribly fierce blow could have inflicted such a wound.

'Well,' said Mannering.

'Not much to "well" about,' said the Toff. 'He knew it was coming, of course.'

'Ye-es,' said Mannering, while the Toff looked closer, without appearing to do so, at a patch of blood on the man's ragged trousers.

It was an odd fact, he noticed, that a piece of sacking lay across the body, covering the torso and the hands and arms, but revealing the legs and shoulder. He wondered why, but there were moments when he preferred not to ask questions. He did so then, as he straightened up and looked at a worried Mannering, a slightly out-of-his-depth-and-showing-it inspector, and the red and almost rheumy face of the doctor – or whom he presumed was a doctor. A big man, apparently in rude health, with rather prominent blue eyes which held an expression almost of insolence. Not a man to like, decided the Toff, while his experience of police-surgeons was that they were either likeable or tolerable. He did not feel tolerant towards Dr. Lowerby, which was odd, for he was a man tolerant in most things.

More: he had seen the man before, but he could not recall where.

Mannering made a patent effort to return to normal.

'Nothing we can do, except get it photographed, I suppose. You'll carry on, Dawbury. Oh—Rolly, this is Inspector Dawbury, who is looking after the case for us, and this is Dr. Lowerby.'

Rollison made the necessary acknowledgments, rather taking to the bluff features and the almost naive puzzlement of Dawbury. When his own name was mentioned he saw Lowerby's eyes widen like those of a man who had received an unpleasant shock. The only people who received shocks upon hearing the Toff's name were those who specialised in doing what they should not.

'Oh, well,' said Lowerby, his voice with a hectoring note, 'nothing more I can do for you, Sir George. Glad to assist any way I can, of course; call on me if necessary.' He nodded bluffly to the trio and walked off. Ascending the side of the quarry by means of a flight of natural steps, he stumbled.

'A pity Dr. Manson's away,' said Dawbury, half to himself and half to Mannering.

'Lowerby isn't your regular man?' asked Rollison.

'No, sir.' Dawbury either did not, or could not, try to conceal a dislike of Lowerby. 'He's acting locum, sir, while the P.S. is away. Ah, but this is a nasty business—not much for a doctor to do, when all's said and done. There's one thing you haven't seen, I think.'

'Oh, yes.' Mannering looked apologetic. 'Move the sack, Dawbury.'

By intent or not, Dawbury whisked the sacking away from the dead man's body to reveal the hands folded at his chest. The Toff, experienced in so many ways of violence, felt a momentary flood of nausea. For the hands were no more than mangled stumps, red and raw as though they had been caught up in a machine. He did not look away, but overcame his repugnance, and then glanced again at the blood on the trousers.

'Distinctly odd,' he said.

'Eh?' – from Mannering.

'I think I know what you mean, sir.' Dawbury glanced at Rollison with a newer respect. 'The damage to the hands was done after the first injury—it looks like that, doesn't it?'

'Very much so,' said the Toff. 'The trousers puzzled me—more wet than dried, the blood there, and it didn't seem to come from the neck. Why kill a man, dispose of his body, take it away again and mangle his hands?'

'Good God!' gasped Mannering.

'Why indeed, sir,' said Dawbury. 'Find the answer to that and we know a lot. Well I'll be superintending formalities, if that's all right with you, Sir George.'

'Yes, yes, carry on,' said Mannering.

He walked with Rollison to the roadway, and stood there indeterminate. And then the Toff saw an expression cross his features – the obstinate expression Mannering revealed on those occasions when his side was fighting a losing battle and he was preparing to do or die at number 11.

'Agree with Dawbury?' he asked abruptly.

'About what?'

'The hands.'

'It's reasonable,' said Rollison non-committally.

'Not so sure,' said Mannering brusquely. 'The hands and trousers were covered with that sacking, and not exposed to the air. That would stop the blood congealing. Wouldn't it?' He pushed his head forward as though challenging Rollison to a denial.

'It could do,' admitted the Toff handsomely. 'Your idea being ... ?'

'Well—supposing they'd wanted some information from him? Good way of getting it would be to make the poor devil suffer—hence his hands. And when they'd got it they cut his throat. I don't say it happened, mind you, but it *does* look possible, doesn't it?'

'I couldn't say no,' admitted the Toff.

He could have said that he considered the theory farfetched and unlikely, but he restrained himself, for Mannering was going to be fond of it. He excused himself from a return trip to the Ridings, and, an hour after he had first started off, set the nose of his Fraser-Nash towards London.

He had made two acquaintances of unusual interest – the body and Dr. Lowerby. It was a remarkable fact that he thought more of Lowerby than of the body until he reached the Chelsea house of Chief-Inspector Horace McNab, of Scotland Yard. McNab, who was proud of his little villa and his small garden, was a burly figure in flannels and open-necked shirt, with leather gloves and secateurs in his hands. As the car drew up he snipped the dead rose off a standard afire with scarlet bloom, and then glanced up with casual interest.

He stopped being casual, and his dour face hardened. There was much that was like granite about McNab, and the sandy eyebrows above his light-blue eyes raised with more than inquisitiveness.

' 'Lo, Mac,' greeted the Toff, and leaned on the garden gate. 'What a thing to be in England now that June is here. Ever entered your roses in a show?'

McNab knew the Toff too well to be gratified.

'Do ye have to be worrying me now?'

'Even out of office hours,' said the Toff cheerfully. 'Apologies and all that. Supposing you act like a little gentleman and ask me in, and uncork a bottle of Black-and-White? You could do with a drink, and I wouldn't say no.'

'I'm not thirsty,' said McNab, drawing off his gloves. 'Ye'd better come in. What's it about—the body that isn't?'

'Wasn't,' said the Toff.

'What're ye meaning?'

'Most undisciplined body that, in the quarry,' said the Toff. 'It was, wasn't, and is. Not a nice corpse, either, Mac, but showing clear evidence of gentlemen with sadistic minds. However' – they had reached the small front room of the house, and McNab was changing his gardening shoes for slippers – 'let it be understood now and for all time that my visit is unofficial and the Sussex people are not consulting the Yard.'

'Well, I can do with a rest,' said McNab.

'A most undutiful remark, seeing there's been murder,' said Rollison. 'A spot more soda, may I? Thanks. Yes, Mac, the body's come back. Any ideas?'

McNab, a more complacent individual at home than at the Yard, where the Toff too often riled him, contemplated the other's sunburned face and submitted: 'Then it hasn't been far away?'

'The world is going mad, for we're agreeing,' marvelled the Toff. 'I don't think it could have been taken far, although a car can travel a tidy distance these days in a matter of hours. On the other hand, they wouldn't take a body fifty miles away to mess up the hands and bring it back. More likely just round the corner, or at least the nearest quiet spot.'

'Mess up what?' asked McNab sharply.

'The hands. Mutilated, Mac. Sir George Mannering had a feeling that they were mutilated before death, as a means of persuasion. It could be, but it's hardly likely, I think. Dawbury—comfortable, competent fellow, Inspector Dawbury—has the other and less melodramatic idea, that it was to make identification difficult. I subscribe to it.'

'Finger-prints,' said McNab; 'he might be on the records.'

'Ye-es. Meaning the killer killed a crook. No, Mac, it's a nasty business, and it isn't made any the better because of certain evidence of a negro and—some suggest—a Chinaman. Any reaction to that?'

'Aweel—no, Rolleeson.' McNab, when thoughtful, lapsed into a more decided accent. 'Will ye be tellin' me—'

Rollison related the questions of the cricketers, the appearance of the Austin 20 and the smaller car, make unknown, the observations of the country policeman, and more details of the body. He did not add that he expected Mannering would be compelled to call for the official assistance of the Yard before long, but McNab accepted that as a probability: he doubted whether the Toff would have come to him unless he had expected an official consultation in the near future.

''Tis a puzzler,' admitted McNab, when the Toff had finished. Humour gleamed in his eyes. 'Ye're not telling me that ye've no ideas of why nor how it happened?'

'Full confession, Mac. I haven't.'

'Why don't ye go back and finish ye're cricket,' demanded the Inspector comfortably, 'and leave it to this man Dawbury?'

'And what would Sir George do then, poor man?'

'Ah, well.' said the Scotsman, 'what is it ye want?'

Rollison chuckled.

'Anything you know concerning anybody who lives in Hersham.'

'I'll have it looked into,' said McNab.

'For which many thanks, Mac. I don't think the hands were cut about to mutilate finger-prints so much as to destroy any and every clue to the man's occupation and habits. Consider: a horny hand could suggest a labourer or a tramp, a smooth palm could mean a clerk or his like, a well-manicured hand a gentleman of some standing. Our mystery was dressed like a tramp—as far as we know he was a tramp. Dawbury and Mannering certainly think so. But the hands, the one proof, are no use to us; he could be a pauper, or a millionaire. Or even a policeman.'

McNab was not amused.

'There's his feet, and his skin.'

'The hands are the better indication,' said Rollison. 'A navvy might take a lot of care with his feet, a clerk might take none at all, and so *ad infinitum*. We can tell by his face whether he had been out of doors a great deal, and he had. But then so have you and so have I?'

'Ay,' said McNab. 'And ye think the man was killed in the quarry and afterwards his hands were disfigured to make it difficult to identify him. And ye've talk of a negro and a Chinaman with a beard.'

'Gentlemen I'd like to locate.'

'I'll see what can be done,' promised McNab.

'While I hope not to be idle,' smiled Rollison, which made McNab grunt. 'We have a nice little problem; there must be several thousand pure-blooded negroes in England, and ten or fifteen thousand—that's a low limit, I fancy—men with beards. Find one of each who know each other, and there you are, or might be. Our Chinaman might only look like one, you know.'

'Do ye know more?' asked McNab sharply.

'Not a thing more than you,' said the Toff amiably. 'But I mean to. We can start from scratch and compare notes, if necessary.'

'Refusing to disclose information leading to the apprehension of a criminal,' said McNab with heavy humour, 'is a crime in itself, Rolleeson, and I'll have ye reminded of it.'

'Allow me a rudimentary acquaintance with the law,' protested the Toff. 'Well, Mac, when Mannering does send an SOS to you people, remember to be grateful to me.'

McNab grunted noncommittally, which was his way of saying that he suspected Rollison was keeping something back.

And for once he was nearly doing the Toff an injustice, for all Rollison had kept to himself was an idea.

Chapter Four

Interest In Dr. Lowerby

Jolly had learned not to appear surprised at anything, and when the Toff entered and demanded dinner he inclined his head and put aside the Toff's library copy of the *Decameron* without apparent reluctance but also without apologising for borrowing it. Rollison, who did not feel in the mood for the *Decameron* or anything heavy, except food, let his mind run riot on the possibilities that the body in the quarry presented. It was, he felt, completely unsatisfactory – the kind of crime with no obvious beginning, and therefore threatening to have no end. Out of the blue a body had been deposited, removed, and replaced.

'Most disconcerting, sir,' said Jolly, when advised.

'You choose your words,' said the Toff absently. 'Yes, disconcerting, but done with reason. The vanishing trick, I mean; all murders are done with reason, even if an insane one. Why should they cart the body away?'

'I leave it to you, sir,' said Jolly.

'Avoid double meanings,' reproved the Toff, 'I'm not in the mood for them. The hands hadn't bled much, or at least I don't think so. The blood on the trousers probably came from hands, after brushing or resting against them. Remarks, Jolly.'

'Were the wrists affected, sir?'

'They were.'

'The vein in the wrist would normally bleed a great deal, or so my knowledge of first-aid suggests, sir.'

'One day you must tell me all you know about first-aid, but for the moment I'll agree with you. The hands and wrists would have bled a lot, if there had been any blood available. Most of it, of course, had gone from the neck. Mannering's all wrong; the mutilation was done afterwards, and was the sole reason for the disappearing trick. But what was the reason for the mutilation?'

'You suggested identification, sir.'

'Yes. of course—Jolly.'

'Sir?'

'Supposing I told you that there had been *two* bodies.'

'It would appear possible, sir.'

'Ye-es. The cyclist was too scared to linger long, and isn't likely to be much use in identification. The police assume that the two bodies are one and the same, and they've every reason to do that. But it isn't a proved fact, Jolly.'

'No, sir. But perhaps a logical assumption.'

'I'm not so sure that I like logic in this case. There's a factor you haven't considered, and Dawbury hasn't considered, and McNab isn't likely to. Why bring the body there first and then remove it for the mutilation? No sense in it; those hands could have been done in a matter of minutes. They—our mystery men, Jolly—were taking a considerable risk, in fact a crazy risk. But if they *wanted* to exchange the bodies, that's a different matter.'

'Yes, sir, but why should they?'

'I am not omniscient,' said the Toff. 'You don't like the theory?'

'I can't see anything to support it, sir.'

'No-o. In that case I must find something. Thing is, if there are two bodies, one is missing and should shortly be discovered. If we get a report about another body at Hersham, the theory gains in credence. Not,' added the Toff, suddenly cheerful, 'that I care a jot whether you agree with me or don't. I'll stay here for the night and go back to Hersham first thing in the morning. Give me a call about seven.'

Jolly said that he would, and did.

Rollison drove down, not fast, for he remained thoughtful, and at eleven o'clock next day reached the Ridings. The teams for the day's match, with a touring side, were already at the nets, but Mannering himself was in his library, and Dawbury was with him. Mannering looked ill-tempered.

'Oh, come in, Rolly—I hoped you'd get back last night.'

'I meant to,' lied the Toff affably. 'Anything else turned up?'

'Not yet. Dawbury here seems to think we'd do well to call on the Yard, but I can't see the need for it yet.'

'We-ell,' drawled Rollison, 'there may not be any need, but this isn't a local job, old man. Or do you think so? I mean, it's not a question of a local resident killed by another local resident. You've got to face the possibility that the body was brought a hundred miles or so—from any one of a dozen counties. I'm all for the Yard, myself.'

'Oh, well,' said Mannering, and then recovered his good temper. 'I'll expect some runs from you for that. All right, Dawbury, I'll see to it right away.'

Outside the library Dawbury hesitated.

'Good of you to help me, Mr. Rollison. Sir George wasn't anxious, and I wouldn't be in an ordinary case, but this isn't *our* murder, as you said. It might have been committed anywhere. Er—I'll be grateful for any help you can give me, sir.'

'It's as good as done,' promised the Toff.

Dawbury thanked him, and the Toff joined the others on the smiling cricket field, and soon lost himself in the grim business of fielding first slip. That was after he had put a sitter on the floor, to the audible amazement of Cozens, at second. It was lunch-time, when the touring-side had built up a good foundation to their score, when he was interrupted again, this time by Dawbury.

'I meant to tell you this morning, sir—about the stuff we found in the tramp's pockets. A bacon sandwich, a few small coins including a French *sou,* and a bit of string, a couple of safety-pins—no papers of any kind.'

'Nothing to help identify him, then?'

'No, sir. But I've found a woman who remembers giving a tramp two bacon sandwiches early yesterday morning, and she's coming to the station to look at the body this afternoon. I'll let you know if she's any help.'

'I've half a mind to come with you.'

'Don't upset Sir George any *more,*' pleaded Dawbury, and the Toff turned down his half-mind.

The woman fainted twice, each time she looked at the dead body, and she could say neither yes nor no. Nor could another countrywoman who had parted – accidentally – with a *sou,* which she had thought to be a halfpenny, to a tramp who had called the night before the bacon-sandwich incident. The tendency of these discoveries made patiently and painstakingly by Dawbury was, the Toff admitted, to suggest that the body was that of a tramp, and not of a man in any other walk of life.

But if a man had killed a tramp, why go to such lengths to prevent him from being identified?

There was no immediate answer to the problem, but the following day precipitated a minor crisis, for the side due to play at the Ridings was forced to scratch at the last moment, and Sir George had the mortification of seeing a peerless June day go by without the pitch being used.

The Toff did not object.

He went into Hersham and – without making himself ostentatious – learned where Dr. Lowerby lived. That was on the outskirts of the town, and as the Toff drove by in his Fraser-Nash he saw Lowerby taking his Morris out of the brick-built garage at the side of the house. Rollison turned his car at the first opportunity, and fifteen minutes later pulled up outside the bank where Lowerby's car was waiting. Lowerby had only that moment gone in.

The Toff followed, pondering among other things on where he had seen Lowerby before: he had a vague conviction that the rheumy, reddish face was not completely unfamiliar.

Two people were already engaging the attention of the two clerks unduly, and Lowerby waited impatiently. He was a man who always looked impatient. The Toff, with intent, approached him from the rear without making a sound, and then said, as if with surprise: 'Hallo—Dr. Lowerby, isn't it?'

Lowerby jumped.

Just for a moment the Toff imagined that he saw what might have been alarm in the doctor's eyes. It disappeared, and Lowerby forced a smile which was not spontaneous but lacked nothing in heartiness.

'Hallo, hallo! Mr. Rollison, isn't it? No cricket today?'

'Match scratched, Chief Constable tearing his hair,' said the Toff amiably. 'What with the murder, and now this, he's having a bad week.'

'Anything developed yet?' Again the Toff imagined that Lowerby's heartiness was forced, that the doctor wished himself a long way from the bank.

'I haven't heard,' he said indifferently. 'I—sorry, the cashier's waiting, I didn't realise—'

He watched without appearing to as Lowerby pushed his paying-in book beneath the grille. There was one cheque in it, and the amount – plain for anyone to see-was a hundred and fifty pounds. A considerable cheque for a country practitioner. The Toff continued to look, and when the cashier stamped the cheque contrived to see that it had been drawn by a Mr. Arnold Chamberlain.

He had no idea what that was likely to mean.

He persuaded the cashier to give him small change for a ten-pound note, this offering reason enough for his call, and followed Lowerby outside. The doctor, however, was already moving, and he did not trouble to wave good-bye.

'Not affable,' murmured the Toff to himself, 'I wonder, Dr. Lowerby, if you've had reason to know of me?'

He slipped into a telephone kiosk nearby and telephoned his flat. Jolly answered in the sharp voice which he used for those admirers of the Toff who were apt to expect to be taken out to lunch when their husbands were safely out of the way.

'I don't want to speak to Mr. Rollison,' said the Toff. 'Dr. Vincent Lowerby, Jolly. Address—Hersham. Try the usual contacts, and see if he means anything. When I say usual, I don't mean the Yard.'

'I see, sir. Shall I call you back?'

'Yes, I'll be at the Ridings.'

He was at the Ridings when he learned from Jolly that, according to a doctor who had been recently released from Parkhurst after sentence for illegal operations, Lowerby was not unknown to certain sections of the criminal fraternity.

'Just how?' asked Rollison.

'He appears to be a little—ah—indiscreet, sir, in the way of prescribing drugs.'

'*What?*'

'That is my information, sir,' said Jolly. 'He has never been convicted, nor do I believe there is any suggestion of malpractice as far as the police or the General Medical Council know, but he was fortunate, I gather, to escape from a drug scandal some five years ago. Dr. Murchison is quite sure it is the same man. At the time Dr. Lowerby had an East End practice, but he moved immediately afterwards to Hersham. That is presumably the reason he moved, sir.'

'Jolly, you're invaluable,' said the Toff.

But he admitted to himself that Jolly might easily have offered an explanation of Lowerby's nervousness. Even an East End doctor five years out of his London practice might have heard of the Toff – and if he had drug-trafficking on his conscience it would explain his nervousness.

It might also explain the large cheque.

On the following morning, Jolly – on the Toff's instructions – arrived at the Ridings. He had found four Arnold Chamberlains in the London Telephone Directory, and visited all of their homes – if homes was the word. Three, said Jolly, were the suburban-town-and-back-each-day type, but the fourth was apparently in a large way of business, selling important furs.

'With a saleroom in Oxford Street, sir, and a warehouse in Lambeth.'

'Have you seen him?'

'No, sir. Discreet inquiries advised me that he was out of town yesterday.'

'Hmmm,' said the Toff. 'Thanks, Jolly. Now get along to Lowerby's place—his morning surgery lasts until half past ten, so he'll be there—and keep your eyes open. For visitors, or any movement on Lowerby's part. If he's nervous of me, he might do foolish things.'

The morning passed uneventfully, with Mannering's side in the field, and Rollison – who was no bowler – rusting in the slips while two powerful batsmen persistently got the ball in the middle of the bat and refused to edge the fast going-away ball which is both the slip field's terror and delight. He was brooding over the past delinquencies of Dr. Vincent Lowerby when the unlikely happened and a ball hummed towards him. He shot his hand out, and the ball stuck. Grinning, he tossed it to the wicket-keeper, and the batsman laughed as he started for the pavilion.

'I thought that caught you napping, Rolly.'

'If only you knew,' smiled Rollison.

Five minutes later they went into lunch, and the Toff prepared to do justice to the meal. He had started on ham and tongue with Russian salad when a footman approached and whispered.

If Jolly suspected that for the third time the Toff's lunch had been spoiled, he showed no signs of it. He was waiting in the lounge, expressionless and yet somehow miserable of mien.

'Don't tell me you've found that body,' said the Toff ill-temperedly.

'No, sir. Dr. Lowerby is leaving for London at one-thirty.'

'Good work. Well, you can stay here until you've told Sir George I've an aching tooth and want it out,' Rollison grinned. 'Ask him, if necessary, to put a sub. in the field for me, and tell him I hope to be able to bat if I'm well enough.'

'Yes, sir,' said Jolly.

The Toff went upstairs and changed into silver greys. Seen by servants but by none of the cricketers, he took the Fraser-Nash from the garage and started towards London. He was on the other side of Dorking when he saw Lowerby's Morris 12 travelling ahead of him, and he passed it at speed, averting his head to avoid recognition.

Unknowingly, Lowerby passed him before they reached town.

From Putney onwards it was easy enough for the Toff to follow without being seen, for he changed his car to a Vauxhall at a garage, warned by phone to expect him, and at half past three he found that Lowerby parked his car in a side-street and walked to the Oxford

Street salerooms of Arnold Chamberlain.

The Toff parked his own car at a nearby garage, and spent ten minutes of intensive activity before returning, and, from a safe vantage point, watched the salerooms. Lowerby's Morris was still near by; the doctor had not yet left Oxford Street, and was not likely to do so without being seen by the Toff.

Chapter Five

Says Chamberlain

The Toff would have been even more interested had he seen Lowerby tap on the door of Mr. Arnold Chamberlain's private office above the Oxford Street shop and enter while 'Come in' was only half uttered.

The fur importer was sitting at a light-oak desk which was littered with trays, papers and telephones. He was smoking a cigar of considerable proportions, and with his horn-rimmed glasses, his prominent chin and his well-developed scowl, he looked what a typical American business man is reputed to be. Lowerby was less concerned with him as a business man, however, than as a buyer of antiques of doubtful value, and of drugs which most people would have called a curse. Moreover, Lowerby was not happy; a child could have seen that, and Chamberlain was certainly not a child.

'Well,' he said breezily, 'I thought everything was fixed up with you, Lowerby; it doesn't do for you to come here too much, you know that. And I'm busy …'

Lowerby was uncertain and nervous of Chamberlain, but much more nervous of the man whom he knew as the Toff, for the Toff's activities in the East End were only too familiar to him.

Lowerby lit a cigarette with fingers which were unsteady and looked as if he could have handled a drink with alacrity. He licked his lips, shifted his eyes from Chamberlain's, and then said sharply: 'No use beating about the bush; I think it's time I dropped the game.

I've been in it long enough, Chamberlain, and—'

He was staring at the fur importer as he spoke, and the expression on the latter's face made him stop short. The look in Chamberlain's eyes was not pleasant.

'So you feel like that, do you? That's a pity, because I've a heap more work for you.'

'I can't handle more,' Lowerby said.

'You can and you will,' said Chamberlain gently. 'I want you, and I'll tell you when you can retire.'

He snapped his fingers sharply, and there was a curious similarity between that sound and another, with which the doctor was not unfamiliar – the firing of a silenced automatic. Looking into the cold blue eyes, Lowerby saw what he disliked. Mr. Chamberlain might be an American, but just then his manner was more of a Big Shot than a Big Business man.

'Maybe it's sinking in,' he drawled. 'No one leaves me until I say so; keep that for future reference. And now you can tell me what's giving you the jitters.'

Lowerby licked his lips, tried to put up a show of confidence, and failed miserably. With a sneer the importer pulled open a cupboard in his desk, took from it a decanter of whisky and a soda-siphon, and pushed them towards his caller.

Lowerby's fingers trembled as he poured out whisky and drank it neat, but it did not immediately steady him. He started to replenish his glass, but Chamberlain covered the top of it quickly.

'That'll do for now. Now what's gotten under your hide? I want the truth, not half of it.'

Lowerby gulped.

'You—you wouldn't understand, old man. You've only been in England for a year, you—you don't know him—'

'Him, is it? I thought the cops had been looking you up. Who is it?' 'A man named Rollison,' muttered Lowerby, and he looked over his shoulder for no reason at all – as if he expected to see the face of the man just behind him. 'He's got a damn-fool nickname—the Toff—and—'

'Sure—and how many bodyguards?'

Lowerby's voice rose.

'It's a damned sight too easy for you to sneer,' he snapped. 'It's all right for you—you haven't met him. But you try and get anyone to tackle him and see what happens. Try Nigger Dougall, or Hi Ling, or any roughneck I put you on to. Tell them the Toff is around and see what happens!'

Chamberlain said: 'Stop screeching, and take another drink. I've never heard of any Rollison, but if he's likely to be a nuisance I'll have him put away. *You* needn't work yourself up over him.'

'Talk's cheap,' snapped Lowerby. 'You don't know Rollison.'

'If he was worth knowing, I would.'

'But Rollison—'

'I'll make inquiries about Rollison. You get back to Hersham, and keep away from the bottle. You're drinking too much, and that's not good for you.'

Lowerby shrugged with a sudden, unexpected change of front. His tongue darted along his fleshy lips, his expression was cunning, almost hunted.

'I'll watch it,' he said. 'But I've got to have something, Chamberlain. I can't stand the strain. I ought to have brought a pinch of snow along with me. I didn't think. Have you got one handy?'

For a moment Chamberlain stared at the red face in front of him, then shrugged. If Lowerby could have guessed at the thought passing through the other's mind he would have been a far more frightened man.

'Surely,' said Chamberlain, almost affably. 'I can let you have a shot, Lowerby—it's yours, anyway.' He took a small paper packet from his desk and tossed it across. Lowerby clutched at it as though he doubted whether it was real and tore it open. He loosened the fine white powder inside with his forefinger, and threw his head back, letting the powder pour into his mouth. Chamberlain watched him expressionlessly.

Ten minutes later, smooth-voiced and smiling, the Dr. Vincent Lowerby who was well known and reasonably popular in Hersham left the office of Arnold Chamberlain, fur importer, and walked steadily down the stairs towards the street and his Morris. His eyes were clear, his manner confident, and his nervousness seemed to have left him.

On the opposite side of the road the Toff was sitting in a Vauxhall saloon, reading an evening paper.

The Toff, nevertheless, looked at Lowerby out of the corner of his eye, and opined to himself that the doctor appeared in excellent spirits. Unaware of the cool appraisal, Lowerby slid into his car and moved off into the stream of traffic entering Oxford Street. The Vauxhall followed him as far as Putney.

There the Toff drove into a garage where he was known with very good reason, and exchanged the Vauxhall for his own Fraser-Nash. He was confident that the doctor had finished his calls for that day, and that he would now drive immediately to Hersham.

'Keeping busy sir?' asked the broken-nosed garage-owner. His profession had been blowing safes until the Toff had persuaded him to live more honestly, and also financed him.

'Always busy,' said the Toff cheerfully. 'But you won't be if you don't hire out better cars than that. Ever heard of a Mr. Arnold Chamberlain, Bill? A fur importer.'

'Noo one on me,' said the ex-crook sorrowfully.

'Well, we can't know everything,' said the Toff. 'Keep your ears to the ground for mention of the gentleman, will you?'

Bill promised that he would, and made inquiries as to the Toff's health, and waved good-bye as the Toff started to break many rules and regulations on his drive back to Hersham.

He went via Esher, thus avoiding Lowerby, who took the main road, and reached the Ridings when six of Sir George Mannering's XI's wickets were down for 154 against a total of over 300. He changed at speed and yet appeared unflurried when he reached the pavilion, to hear Mannering's gasp of mingled relief and condemnation.

'What the deuce have you—'

'Peace on you,' said the Toff. 'I've been busy, all for the love of you. Hallo, Toby's out. Who's that fast merchant?'

'Everitt, of Sussex. Get your pads on, and if you don't get some runs …'

The Toff smiled and obliged. The task of scoring a hundred and forty-odd runs in forty minutes was well beyond him, but he was on the way when stumps were drawn, and the danger of losing was averted. On such a day he felt capable of challenging Hutton, for he was pleased with his efforts in London. Sir George, who had a childish horror of losing any of his week's matches, was sufficiently pleased to grant forgiveness and ask no questions, and he made no demur when the Toff assured a sceptical gathering that his appointment had been with his dentist.

Early the next day, when he had ample time to get back to the Ridings, the Toff called at the Putney garage again. The ex-safebreaker had some news for him, although none as far as he knew of Arnold Chamberlain.

'About five minutes after you'd gorn,' said Bill, 'a bloke came to know if I'd dekko'd a man with a big Vauxhall. He never see it in the garich, but I reckon you must 'a' been follered yesterday.' Bright Cockney eyes regarded the Toff knowingly.

'Your reckoning's good,' allowed the Toff, and he felt thoughtful. He had suspected the possibility of a shadow from the Oxford Street establishment, believing it unlikely that Lowerby would be careless. 'Just what did you say?'

'I told 'im,' said Bill, with evident self-appreciation, 'that you 'ad an orffice upstairs, and yer Vauxhall was in the garich, but it 'adn't been art yesterday. Okay?'

'Okay. What kind of a gentleman?'

'Little cove, with a squint.'

The Toff took from his pocket a cutting from a week-old newspaper, recently taken from a newspaper file. Jolly had discovered it, and it showed a passable likeness of an Arnold Chamberlain as "a new influence in the fur market". Jolly's habit of reading the City page was one of his most unlikely traits.

'Any likeness?' asked the Toff.

'No,' said Bill emphatically, 'not a glim. When I sez a squint I means a squint.'

'So that,' reflected the Toff to himself, 'means that Chamberlain or Lowerby employs a man or men, and as it was on Chamberlain's home ground it looks like him. Lowerby may have reported the Vauxhall, of course.' Aloud, 'The man with the squint saw that I was active yesterday, and followed me for my sins, William.'

Bill grinned, rubbing a stubbly chin with a spatulate forefinger and winking bright-blue eyes.

'They'll 'ear from you, I reckon.'

'Which is a nice faith,' acknowledged the Toff. 'I hope so. Get in touch with friends of yours in the fur trade, Bill; they'll know if Chamberlain does much genuine business. No burglaries, mind you, no fur-warehouse exploits; they're my preserves until further notice.'

'I'll give the boys the wire,' said Bill.

'Do. Now then, a negro and a Chinaman working together. Does it mean anything?'

'They don't mix much,' said Bill. 'Colours never do, mister, but you don't need tellin' that. An' I ain't been around much, seein' I'm earning a livin' even if you don't like me Vauxhall. But I'll slip down "Steam Packet" way this arternoon.'

'Stout fellow,' said the Toff. 'Give everyone my love, but don't tell them I'm busy.'

'Okay,' said Bill with relish.

The match at the Ridings was not important, and Rollison telephoned, announced developments on the matter of the body, and received Mannering's grudging admission that the murder-hunt was more important than cricket. Thus released for the day, the Toff talked again with Jolly, started further inquiries and – finding a remarkable absence of information about the fur importer and the two men he was anxious to see – decided to investigate again through McNab. Meanwhile he tried to remember where he had seen Lowerby before he had met the doctor at Hersham.

Of course, if the man had had a West End practice, that might be explanation enough.

But his impression was that the encounter had been more recent, and his inability to recall it annoyed him. He retired from the effort after half an hour, and pondered all that he knew.

A Chinaman, a negro, a little man with a squint, Mr. Arnold

Chamberlain and Dr. Vincent Lowerby. Being honest, he acknowledged that as yet there was no direct connection between the first two and the last three. He was working entirely on the assumption that Lowerby knew more about the dead tramp than appeared on the surface.

'Once find that connection,' he confided to Jolly, 'and I shall be a happier man. Put this in an envelope, Jolly, and post it to our Arnold.'

Jolly took one of the decorated visiting-cards, sealed it and addressed it, and posted it in time to catch an early collection.

Some three hours after, thanks to the speed of the Post Office delivery system, Chamberlain tore open the envelope. Then he stared at the side that presented itself first – the pencilled drawings of a top hat, a monocle, and a cigarette-in-holder. He turned the card over, and then jumped as if stung – which was the effect the Toff's card had on many people.

Chamberlain did not know that it was his first experience of that queer method of attack which the Toff called psychological terrorism. He simply felt the sudden stab of surprise.

And – being a man of quick decisions – he decided abruptly what to do with the Toff.

Chapter Six

McNab Obliges

Sylvia Sanderson recovered consciousness without immediately remembering the horror through which she had passed. Her head ached abominably, her mouth was parched and unpleasant, the result of the chloroform. She lay on a camp-bed for half an hour, in a stupor that was only half wakefulness, and without realising that she was bound to the bed.

As the throbbing in her head eased a little she stirred, and suddenly memory returned, a sudden stabbing recollection of the horror of the moment when her father had been murdered. It had a nightmare vividness, and made her scream, although only a faint muttering passed her lips.

Screaming, she struggled, and realised that she could not move.

It did not immediately stop her from trying. In a panic she strained against the cords at her wrists, vainly she tried to kick those at her ankles free. It was gloomy where she was, although not quite dark, and the small room was hot and stuffy; she was sticky with sweat.

Quietness returned, if not real calm.

After a while she realised the danger of letting her mind dwell on the horror, for as she saw that murder in her mind's eye a shiver ran through her body, she felt a rising nausea in her stomach. She tried to force herself to think more calmly, to remember other things.

He father had been worried of late, although he had scoffed when she had said so.

And Chamberlain, the man she had never liked, had sent him to the house.

Chamberlain …

Panic threatened again when she thought of the negro and the Chinaman, but either she was too physically exhausted for it to gain a complete hold, or her strength of will was enabling her to visualise it without losing her self-control. She could remember every word the men had said.

'We've found yuh, okay.'

Had they been looking for her father?

Had they known beforehand where he was likely to be?

Or had the Rolls-Royce been followed?

She tried to think of what would happen. No one knew where they had come that morning, as far as she was aware. Except Chamberlain, of course. But her father had been killed, the police would discover that, and she …

They *must* find her.

She shivered as the possibility that they would not passed through her mind. Then she tried to imagine why she should be kept there, whether she played any part in the conspiracy against her father. It seemed quite certain that she had been living with him without realising that he was in danger, that his murder had been the result of a gradual building-up of circumstances. An odd, uncommunicative but lovable man, James Sanderson.

She bit her lips suddenly, felt tears rising to her eyes.

She did not know how long she cried, nor how many minutes or hours passed before the door was opened, and a man whom she could see only vaguely because of the semi-darkness released her hands, let her drink water, put sandwiches of some kind on a chair next to the bed, and then went out. Her hands were free, but ominous in her ears was the sound of the key turning in the lock.

That silent visit made the room more uncanny, more eerie, and it increased her fear. But by bringing her face to face with the danger that might threaten her it dimmed the horror of the murder, although she did not fully realise it just then.

The affair of the murdered tramp – 'tramp' assumed by the police and the Press, even if the Toff was still inclined to his own theory, and doubted whether it was the body of a vagrant – was one, the Toff would say, of delayed action. Not his first nor his last of the kind, although usually he sailed into his opponents earlier in the chase. Having no known opponents was a distinct disadvantage.

Some hope came with the call of Bill, from the Putney garage, late on the evening when he had cried off the match at Hersham. Jolly, who appeared to consider some of the Toff's friends as proof that the Toff's soul was in jeopardy, announced a Mr. Smith gloomily.

'Usher Mr. Smith in,' said the Toff.

Bill advanced, mufflered and breezy, shook hands heartily, and yet sat on the edge of a chair.

'I don't mind if I do,' he said when the Toff suggested beer. 'Um. You know a thing or two, you do. *That* didn't come out of no four-ale bar.'

'A compliment for you, Jolly,' said the Toff, and Jolly – standing by the door – forgot himself so far as to grimace. 'Jolly looks after all the beer here, Bill. I look after the wines.'

'Ain't got no time for short drinks,' said Bill with complete aplomb. He refused a Virginia 3, and rolled shag in a soiled cigarette-paper. 'I bin snoopin', sir.'

'And I gather with purpose.'

'Right,' said Bill, and lit his cigarette with enjoyment. 'Dougall an' 'I Ling, that's them.'

'"Them" being who?'

'Darkie an' the Chink,' said Bill with satisfaction. 'I noo I'd find 'em if you wasn't imagering them. They 'angs out at the 'Steam Packet' a lot by night. Coupla nasty bits o' work, I believe. Nigger Dougall, they calls 'im. Come over from the 'Ook some munce ago, an' they've bin layin' low.'

The Toff translated silently.

Nigger Dougall and Hi Ling spent a considerable time at the 'Steam Packet', an East End pub of unsavoury reputation and notorious friendliness towards wanted men. They had reached this country from Holland, and for some months they had not been active – as far as their few acquaintances knew.

'Bill, you're a treasure,' praised the Toff. 'Nothing else?'

''Ow much do *you* want fer yer pint?' demanded Bill, grinning and revealing the gaps between his strong but yellowing teeth.

'Make it two pints,' said the Toff. 'So that's the lot?'

'On the up-an'-up, I don't know anuvver thing.'

'Right,' said the Toff. 'Keep that ear to the ground, and now run along and try to make the engine of that Vauxhall go everytime you press the self-starter, instead of once in three.'

Bill departed, confiding to Jolly that he was a card, he was, and the Toff looked at his watch, to find that it was half past eight. He called the Yard, and learned that McNab had been working late. Yes, he would see Rollison, but not to dispense free drinks.

The Toff had already made a tentative inquiry about Arnold Chamberlain. Some folk would have been surprised that he kept in such close touch with the police, but that was his practice unless he had good reason to believe that he could get better and quicker results. He was allowed to walk unattended to the Chief Inspector's office, to find McNab, of the four usual occupants, the only one on duty. McNab pushed back a file of papers.

'An' what now, Rolleeson?'

'Anything of the negro?' asked the Toff.

'Not a thing. Are you sure ye're talking of folk who really exist?'

'Reasonably sure, Mac. A Sussex policeman saw them, when all's said and done.'

McNab's grunt might have expressed his opinion of Sussex policemen.

'You have'na yourself?'

'I have not.' Rollison hitched his trousers up as he leaned back in his chair, and went on, 'You've been called in officially by the Sussex people, haven't you?'

'Och, yes, I've been there most of the day.'

'Nothing new?'

'Nothing. Why *should* they kill a tramp?'

'Now come, that's my question,' protested the Toff. 'What's the medical evidence?'

'The hands were done after death,' said McNab. 'It's fairly obvious, Rolleeson, not that I think much of your Lowerby.' He sniffed. 'Lowerby had a London practice once, maybe you recall it.'

'He was before my time.'

'Maybe it was as well for him,' said McNab. ''Tis a poor doctor that feeds himself with drugs.'

So McNab knew that much, thought the Toff.

'A poor one indeed,' he agreed. 'All right, Mac. Now, Chamberlain. Have you looked him up?'

'Nothing against the man at all,' said McNab, not without satisfaction. 'He's an American who has applied for naturalization papers, and gives a good account of himself in America. There are no black marks against him over there, ye ken. He's managing director of a fur-importing company, and owns ninety per cent of the shares himself. A *very* straightforward gentleman.'

'How long has he been trading over here?'

'Ten months, and he bought the business as a going concern. He does most of his trading with Central Europe, Rolleeson, a little with Canada, and a wee bit with China and Japan.'

'Quite cosmopolitan,' reflected the Toff, and proffered cigarettes. 'A good, profitable business, you would say?'

'It appears so.'

'Hmm. Lucky man who can make good profits out of trading abroad so much,' reflected the Toff. 'Central Europe—on a perpetual war basis. China and Japan, ditto. He must do a lot with Canada to make up for his losses! Don't mind me, Mac, it's just my naturally suspicious mind.'

'I can see the point,' admitted McNab, 'but there's nothing against the man.'

'So I gathered. Ten months or so is a short time for an alien to stay here and start thinking of naturalization, isn't it?'

'Ye-es, but he's been to and from England a great deal, and he's none so poor. Mind ye, I'm not saying he'll get his papers, but he's applied for them, and there's no known reason why he shouldn't get through.'

'Thumbs up for Arnold,' smiled the Toff. 'Odd thing. Mac, but I haven't met the gentleman yet.'

'I can't imagine him being sorry about that,' said McNab dryly.

'Age is sharpening your power of rejoinder! Well—'

'Why are ye so interested in Chamberlain?' McNab cocked his head as the Toff pushed his chair back.

'Because I'd a peculiar idea,' he said, 'that he might have been a friend of our tramp. And might not, of course. Have you learned anything about that poor beggar?'

'Not a thing,' said McNab. 'We have'na his name, nor anything aboot him; he might ha' been sent fra' heaven to gi' me a pain in the neck. Me and Dawbury.'

'Now that,' said the Toff, from the door and sorrowfully, 'was very nearly blasphemy, and you should be ashamed of yourself. Will you meet me on a point of policy?'

'I'll promise ye nothing before I know what it is.'

'That won't take long. If Chamberlain's as clever as I think he might be, he'll smell a C.I.D. man a mile off, and I'd hate to think I'd given him cause to.'

'Ye really think he's in the business?'

'Yes,' said the Toff without hesitation. 'But it may be a very long shot. Too many mights and mays, I'll agree, but there it is. If I *knew* anything I wouldn't be telling you about it, and you've no official reason for going after him.'

'That's so. All right, Rolleeson, I'll not have him watched.'

'What more could I want?' asked Rollison. 'Speaking generally and not about this business, what's causing the official mind the most concern these days?'

McNab sniffed.

'There's more drugs about than we like, but there always is. Outside of that, things run quietly.'

The Toff's eyes were brooding, for dope was the one thing which he detested most. A man who peddled drugs murdered and ruined lives more surely than any killer. And there was Lowerby, whom McNab did not know had once done more than take the stuff.

He nodded, almost affably.

'Business as usual then,' he said. 'We ought to thank our tramp for variety.'

A moment later he was gone, and McNab had a memory of a brief wave of farewell and a smile at once genial and brilliant; and of the lean, confident figure of the Toff.

McNab was a little uneasy, apart from the Toff.

The underworld was rumbling like a volcano coming to life after years of quiet, although the volcano of human vice covered by the Wapping, Shadwell, Mile End and other areas had been quiet for only a few months. There was a threat of an eruption, a thing he could feel but not talk about, because it was not yet a fact.

And then McNab glimpsed what the Toff had seen a few days before.

The tide of crime had been at its lowest ebb, London had been sweltering beneath the summer heat, too indolently busy for serious crime – on the surface. But all the time the volcano had been rumbling the dope had been peddled, other things of the like nature had been brewing. With the spadework done so quietly that only the vaguest of rumours had filtered through to Scotland Yard, so quietly that even the Toff had heard nothing of it, the surface threatened to crack.

Afterwards the Inspector was appalled by the accuracy of his thoughts that day. The Toff, without knowing it, almost made McNab feel fey.

Meanwhile, and in spite of his apparent agreement, but because he was a policeman and policemen worked to routine, he put two of the Yard's best men to shadow Mr. Arnold Chamberlain from America.

Which was precisely what the Toff had wanted.

Chapter Seven

Delayed Action

Nigger Dougall was the son of a negro sailor and a white woman, and he had inherited the vices of Africa and the West, plus not a few of his own invention. He was more black than white, a monster of a man, with a neck as thick as many men's thighs, a pair of thick, wet and red lips, a flattened nose, tiny eyes with yellow 'whites', and the physical strength of a gorilla. His voice was thick and deep, typically negroid, and he claimed with some justification to have the cunning of a hundred foxes. He had once led a terror-squad in Chicago, until G-men days; thereafter he roamed many countries with one or two of his best men by him. In London he patronised the 'Steam Packet', which pub in Dockland he had bought with stolen money – a purchase so cunningly contrived that none knew him for the owner. Yet in London, until Chamberlain had come, he had felt his wings were clipped.

Hi Ling, on the other hand, had never possessed wings.

He had one thing in common with Nigger: a deceased white mother. His father had been a crafty Chinese merchant, so that he mixed the vices of the Orient and Occident, and needed no inventions of his own. His speciality was smuggling, but until the arrival of Arnold Chamberlain he had never smuggled dope into England. He realised that in the little island dope and a Chinaman were considered synonymous terms, and he had preferred to take smaller profits from safer game.

Arnold Chamberlain, apparently fresh from America, with a first-hand knowledge of gunmen as good as Nigger's, a ready-made business under his control, and a blameless reputation, had started to make big money, so he had said, by applying U.S.A. methods to U.K. prices.

Actually he had not come from America.

He had applied for naturalization in the name of a man who had died mysteriously, but that man's death is no part of this story. He was phony from start to finish, but believed that no one in England would suspect that.

He had learned of Nigger, and had hired him; he had thus heard of Hi Ling, and had chartered the Chinaman's cargo-boats for the transport of furs, and for other things. He paid good money and he got good service, and until Lowerby's visit he had been well content.

On the morning following the visit to Oxford Street of Dr. Vincent Lowerby, Chamberlain went in his car to some Turkish baths in Aldgate, and left the premises five minutes later, minus horn-rimmed glasses and blue pince-nez, and wearing a tawny-grey wig. He travelled from Aldgate to Roger's Comer, a tram junction near the 'Steam Packet', by tram. At the junction he alighted and hurried towards the docks and the 'Steam Packet', followed at a distance by the man with the squint. Mr. Chamberlain had not yet learned the habit of travelling unguarded.

He pushed through the swing-doors of the saloon bar, ordered a whisky, grunted at the barman's attempted pleasantries, and five minutes later left the squalid, low-ceilinged pub. The man with the squint was fifty yards along the road, and nodded as Chamberlain looked towards him, offering a clear bill. It was safe enough to re-enter the pub and to see Dougall and Hi Ling.

Both of these gentlemen were waiting. The black, perspiring mountain of a negro and the thin, tall under-sized Chinaman presented a contrast in the absurd; although Chamberlain did not notice it.

The room below the 'Steam Packet' was wide and airy, and a luxury hotel would not have scorned its pile carpet its lounge chairs, its oak-panelled walls. The two crooks liked comfort in their hide-out, and they had achieved it.

The Chinaman, smiling and suave, dispensed whisky and bowed low as he lifted his glass, looking odd in his European clothes. Nigger, as always, seemed about to burst his seams. He spoke first, his voice thick and husky.

'Well, suh,' he said. 'Yuh'll be wanting us again?'

'The last trip was quite satisfactory, yes?' murmured Hi Ling. He was the quieter, more self-effacing man of the two – and infinitely more dangerous in a battle of wits.

'Couldn't have been better,' admitted Chamberlain. 'I'll say you know your jobs. The furs were warehoused this morning, and the other stuff taken out. But I've not come on the usual line; I've got another job like Sanderson's.'

'So.' Hi Ling was expressionless. Nigger's tongue ran along his lips, not pleasantly.

'Dat was a good job,' he growled. 'An' easy. De tramp – I came behind him as he sat against a milestone in de half-dark, and I got behind him an' grabbed him. De hands is always best, Mr. Chamberlain, yessuh, dey can't squawk.'

'Probably you'll have another opportunity of using them,' said Chamberlain gently, 'and one even more important.'

'You need have no worry,' murmured Hi Ling. 'Who is your friend, Mr.—'

'Never mind the Misters,' said Chamberlain. 'I know you and you know me, and that's okay by all of us,' He leaned back, smiling. 'Careful all the time, see, it pays.'

'But de guy you want croaked?' said Nigger.

Chamberlain leaned back in his chair and eyed them evenly. He knew they represented the worst elements of London's underworld, that although they had not ostensibly been busy they knew their ground from A to Z. He knew that both men had murders by the dozen on their consciences, that they snuffed out human life with as little concern as a candle; murder was in the way of business.

Yet Lowerby had said they would shy from Rollison.

'It is a man,' said Chamberlain, 'who has been proving a nuisance, and might prove more. I think—I'm not sure—that he has some idea that I knew Sanderson—'

'Certainly he must go,' murmured Hi Ling gently.

'His name,' said Chamberlain carelessly, 'is Rollison or Rollson …'

As he spoke, even as the name came out, while he watched the two men in front of him, he saw their expressions alter. He saw Dougall lick his lips furtively and the Chinaman's suave smile disappear, as if a shadow entered those slanting eyes.

The air of the room seemed chill,

'The Toff!' murmured Hi Ling, but his voice was very low. 'I begin to see.'

'I said Rollison,' Chamberlain said.

'De same guy,' said Dougall. He poked a small cigar into his mouth and lit it, as if wanting something to do. He started to move about the apartment, looking everywhere but at Chamberlain. 'See here, mistah, you are asking for trouble if you try and get that guy. The Toff ain't so easy.'

'A *most* dangerous gentleman,' murmured Hi Ling.

The man who had never heard of the Toff remembered a visiting-card, and then felt a sudden anger.

'Goddam it, he's a man! What's scaring you?'

There was a short, almost dangerous, silence. Hi Ling's face was smooth and expressionless, there was no smile on his lips. Nigger Dougall's ham-like fists were clenched, and his voice was sharp.

'Listen, we do your work and you pay us money—but we ain't paid to be talked to like that. Understand? Maybe you think we're scared, maybe you don't. Which ever it is, don't say it, we don't like hearing you.'

The silence came again and Chamberlain broke it, but with an effort. He sensed the reason for the change of front, and he knew that Lowerby had spoken the truth; the Toff was a man to be feared because he was a man who was feared.

'Aw, shucks, no offence was meant,' he said. 'I'm not hurting your feelings. But if this man gets going, and no one'll put him away, we're not on Easy Street.'

'We could try,' Hi Ling said, 'because the money in this work is good, *very* good. But for this, for the Toff, who is very good also, the money must be even better.'

'Shut your trap!' grunted Nigger. 'We can't get him, it ain't safe.'

Chamberlain's eyes travelled from the negro to the Chinaman, feeling more of the influence of the Toff than he had dreamed possible in so short a time. He knew then that the man had to go, there was no alternative.

'I'll pay you five hundred pounds.'

'Jeeze!' Nigger was startled. 'Dat's—'

'Each?' said Hi Ling gently. 'Each, and we will agree.'

Chamberlain swallowed hard, but did not hesitate for long.

'You know how to drive a deal. Okay, five hundred apiece.'

'It is good money,' said Hi Ling softly, and as he rubbed his hands together it was possible to imagine the long, wide sleeves of a gown that he might have worn had he been born five hundred years before – or even worn today had he been ten thousand miles away. His yellow face, with the straggly beard that had made such an impression on several minds, was quite expressionless, and his almond-shaped eyes regarded Chamberlain with a kind of impersonal benevolence. 'Yes, good money indeed, but I would be pleased to think we shall earn it quickly.'

'We don't oughta touch it,' growled Nigger.

Chamberlain, despite his grey wig and his pince-nez, looked very much himself at that moment – and he also looked annoyed.

'What *is* this talk about Rollison? Who's he?'

'Who is the devil?' Hi Ling said, and then shrugged and smiled. 'You say we exag'rate, and maybe it is so, but Rollison is well known, he has a way few others have.'

'What is he, a private dick?'

'Alas, no. That, perhaps, is the trouble.' Hi Ling's English was nearly perfect, only a faint singsong intonation characterised it, and the odd use of some words. 'He is rich, he works not for money, and he can buy friends and information, so many friends, so much info'mation. It is true, Dougall?'

'I'll say it's true.' Nigger hunched his big shoulders: the seams of his coat threatened once again to burst. 'I'm not aimin' to have de Toff runnin' on my tail. I guess we'll move quick, maybe we'll get through.'

'We have not fought the Toff,' said Hi Ling softly. 'It is perhaps the sign that we should begin.'

'Goddam you!' snapped Chamberlain. 'Stick a knife in his ribs, or use those hands Nigger's so fond of. He's human, isn't he?'

'It is said,' Hi Ling murmured. 'You do not know, you cannot know until you have met him. *That* is so, I give my word.'

It was uncannily similar to Lowerby's remark, but there was no chance that Hi Ling was reaching a stale of nervous prostration through drugs or whisky. The negro might have superstitious fears, but Hi Ling was cold and implacable, a man of fact, not fancy.

Chamberlain rubbed his chin.

'I guess I'd like to meet this man.'

'How did you come to learn of him?' demanded Hi Ling.

'A friend told me,' said Chamberlain shortly. 'And then Rollison sent a card.'

'With small drawings?'

'Some crazy pencilled markings, yes, I—'

'You tore it up,' said Hi Ling, and he laughed mirthlessly. 'The first one, it is always torn up. You will meet him, I can assure you of that.'

'What?'

'First he send his card, then he comes,' said Hi Ling. 'It is the way of Rollison. But of course, we shall be busy at once, it is possible he dies first.'

'Me, I think we should back right out've this,' growled Dougall. 'I'm reckoning, sah—'

He stopped, for a buzzer set somewhere in the wall burred out and made Chamberlain jump. The eyes of the negro and the Chinaman turned towards the door. Above it they saw a small green light, while Chamberlain followed their gaze and frowned.

'What's that?'

'A warning when the first stair is touched,' said Hi Ling. 'The green light, it means a friend who knows the way to enter is coming. Enter, please.' He raised his voice as a tap came on the door, and waited. Chamberlain rubbed his chin, and said with evident admiration: 'You do take care. I—'

He stopped, and Nigger swore. Only Hi Ling seemed unaffected by the little man who entered. A normal enough little man, in shirt-sleeves and a green baize apron, a mop of reddish hair and the sharp features typical of so many Cockneys. It was not his general appearance so much as the expression in his face – an expression of either fear or alarm, or both.

In a large and knuckly right hand he held a small slip of pasteboard, as if afraid it would bite him.

'Tommy, why do you come?' asked Hi Ling gently.

'A—a cove gimme this,' said Tommy, and handed the card with evident relief to Hi Ling. 'It wasn't Rawlison, you don't 'ave to worry about that; 'e slipped it inter me 'and—'

'Rollison!' snapped Chamberlain.

Hi Ling turned and shrugged his shoulders, and flicked the card across to Chamberlain. It was identical with that which the fur importer had already received, except that across the proper side were scrawled the words:

Who owns the Austin?

'You can go,' Hi Ling said to the barman. He turned to Dougall, who was darting his tongue along his lips, and shrugged. 'We have no choice now, my friend, the Toff knows us; it is the Toff or us.'

'But how?' demanded Chamberlain sharply. 'How'd he know you? How did—'

'So many questions, so few answers,' said the Toff.

His voice floated from the door, which was partly opened, but all they saw of him was his gun and the right hand that held it. Chamberlain clenched both hands and thumped them on the desk, even though he did not recognise the drawling mockery in his tone, nor the lilt that was never far away.

'Hands right away from pockets, please,' continued the Toff as amiably. 'Especially you, Hi Ling; that little knife of yours slips so easily.' He came through and kicked the door to behind him. He was dressed in a dinner-jacket suit, and on his head was a top-hat set at a slightly rakish angle. From his left eye dangled a monocle – on such expeditions he used one, but the glass inside was plain: it was part of the legend he had built about himself. He was smiling and debonair, and yet he created an impression of restrained force; all that was dynamic about the Toff revealed itself then.

'Why, yuh—' snarled Nigger.

'Because I wanted to meet you all,' said the Toff genially. 'Don't slip, my friend, I always have disliked black corpses. And who is our grey-haired gentleman with so benevolent an aspect?' He regarded Chamberlain with mocking appraisal, and Chamberlain felt himself sweating, forgot that he was wearing his grey wig, and that in other ways he differed from his normal appearance.

'It is always the pleasure to meet you, *Mister* Rollison.' Hi Ling had taken the intrusion more calmly than the others, but his eyes were narrowed to mere slits, and his right hand was not far from his pocket.

'Mutual accord then?' murmured the Toff. 'I wonder. I also wonder why you killed the tramp.'

With the last words his voice dropped, was low-pitched and cold – and accusing. He saw Chamberlain flinch, saw Hi Ling's eyes flare with a quick fury – and he saw Dougall jump.

The negro moved with a lightning speed, swearing as he leapt, murder within him. He reached the Toff, who did not shoot – for it was the Toff's preference to do the unexpected.

Hi Ling's right hand moved to his pocket.

The Toff side-stepped and Dougall's whirling fists missed him. He cracked a right to the negro's stomach, and the gasp echoed through the room. He ducked – and from Hi Ling a knife hurtled, its shining blade curving a vicious arc through the air. As the blade struck the wall and splintered, the Toff put out his foot and sent the negro sprawling. And then he stood quite still by the closed door, his gun pointing towards Hi Ling, who was standing disarmed and helpless, and Chamberlain.

And then Chamberlain flashed a gun from his shoulder-holster.

Chapter Eight

Says The Toff

It was a foolish thing for any man to do, although in extenuation there was the fact that Chamberlain had never seen the Toff in action. It seemed impossible that he could handle Dougall, dodge the knife, and yet be in time to counter shot for shot. The Toff's speed of movement was one of those things in which no one believed until they had seen it. Then, of course, they magnified it out of all recognition, and it attained a quality of fantasy.

Two shots snapped out.

Both guns were silenced, there was little sound as two stabs of flame a foot long spat towards each other. Chamberlain's was a fraction of a second behind the Toff's; his bullet travelled upwards, for the hand that held the gun was suddenly filled with an excruciating pain, and the gun went flying from his grasp, struck by the Toff's bullet.

The Toff moved aside, safe from the dazed Dougall, whose head had cracked against the wall and was not proof against plaster-covered brick and mortar.

'Not friendly,' said the Toff, 'especially at a first meeting. But I won't insist on apologies. Go back to the table there, Hi Ling, Dougall, get after him. You needn't move, my grey-haired gunman. How long have you been away from Sing-Sing?'

Chamberlain licked his lips.

Dougall picked himself up unsteadily and joined Hi Ling by the table. It was Hi Ling who answered; the Chinaman was going to present the greatest danger, thought the Toff.

He could have forced the issue then.

He could have sent word for McNab, and the negro and the Chinaman might have been identified. When the police started their routine inquiries, much would come to light. But the Toff was by no means sure that the circumstantial evidence so far available would hang either man – and he was quite sure they both needed hanging.

Nor could he be sure that he would discover just what Chamberlain and Lowerby were doing.

They were dangerous when at liberty, but liable to make mistakes – and at that time the Toff knew of no one but himself who might be a likely victim of their attentions. He wanted to scare them now – and with Dougall and the grey-haired man probably that would not be difficult – and force them afterwards into mistakes that would mean a complete capitulation.

Hi Ling said softly: 'You are quick, my friend. Too quick for some.'

'Much too quick,' said the Toff, 'although I doubt whether you meant it quite that way. How long have you been working with Arnold Chamberlain?'

It was not a good break for the Toff.

He had not seen Chamberlain, he had no idea that the man with the grey hair was the fur importer. And all he gathered from the expressions on their faces was that they knew of the man. He saw sweat beading the gunman's forehead, and it pleased him.

'How long?' he repeated. 'Or could I be mistaken?'

'You are quite mistaken,' Hi Ling said evenly. 'The name means nothing to us, Rollison.'

'No? A pity. I don't like guessing wrong. However …' He leaned back against the door negligently, and the gun seemed to drop towards the floor, although none of them showed signs of taking advantage of it. In the brief *mêlée* his hat had reached a more rakish angle, and his monocle had dropped from his eye. Neither fact worried him.

'However,' he repeated, 'I have some home-truths. A tramp, some say, was murdered, and the murderers aren't far from here. One day they will swing. There is a lot of dope around in London, and that might not concern the tramp, but the pedlars aren't far from here either. Seeing that they'll swing, they can't serve fifteen years, but they can be made to feel sorry for themselves. Very sorry,' he added gently. 'Am I understood?'

Quite clearly he was understood.

But there was something else in the face of Dougall, if not the others, that puzzled him. He felt as he watched them that they knew something that he had not touched, that they were waiting for yet further indirect accusations. It was an unpleasant feeling in its way. It suggested he had not plumbed the depths of their villainy nor the limits of their activities, and it worried him. From the first he had known that the association of a negro and a Chinaman would be blacker than most; now he had proof of it, but not a proof to serve in any court of law.

'Words, they are so cheap,' said Hi Ling.

'Aren't they?' said the Toff, and he had to force himself not to show his annoyance – an essential plank in his psychological warfare was to appear unruffled and unperturbed whatever the circumstances, whatever he was feeling. 'Both sides, Hi Ling. There are, of course, other things.'

He saw the grey-haired man stiffen.

Dougall licked his lips.

'Just what?' asked Hi Ling softly.

'A matter,' said the Toff, 'for further discussion; I haven't time now. But it's there.' He paused, and then he shrugged and said easily, 'That other body.'

It was Dougall who let him see that he was near if not right on the mark. Chamberlain had recovered, and Hi Ling had lost his self-control only for a brief spell. The Toff did not let them see that Dougall had in part betrayed himself, but laughed.

The laugh was light, but made it seem as if the Toff was thoroughly enjoying himself – which, perhaps, he was. It was the kind of thing that was more valuable than quick shooting or heavy punching. It worried the other side and would keep worrying them.

He waved, and opened the door without looking away from the trio. He stepped out, and the door closed with a sharp click.

'The—' swore Dougall, and rushed at the door as if he would break it down. Chamberlain had risen from his chair, and Hi Ling was about to speak sharply to Dougall.

He had no need.

The door opened as abruptly as it had closed. The wooden panel rapped sharply against the negro's head, and Dougall dropped back with a grunt of pain. The Toff beamed.

'Too bad,' he drawled; 'it would be such a relief if you could always be sure where I was, wouldn't it? My love to Chamberlain.'

He closed the door again, and meant it this time. Before Hi Ling could summon Tommy the barman to see where the Toff went, the Toff was in the ill-lighted streets outside and walking with speed away from the 'Steam Packet'.

With the confirmation that he had left the pub, which he had contrived to enter unostentatiously by a side-door, the atmosphere in the converted cellar at the 'Steam Packet' eased. Chamberlain lit a cigar, scraping the match viciously against the side of the box.

'So that's Rollison, and he still thinks he's clever.'

'You do not agree?' asked Hi Ling.

'He didn't know me,' snapped Chamberlain. 'The goddamned fool would have the wind taken out of his sails if he knew he'd been speaking to "Chamberlain". I—'

'It was a mistake,' Hi Ling admitted, 'but one easy to make. Do not believe Rollison has a habit of making them. Certainly he knows you are connected with the Sanderson murder.'

'No one knows Sanderson is murdered!' snapped Chamberlain. 'Keep quiet about that!'

'We are safe here, we will not be overheard,' said Hi Ling.

'Safe? *He* got in—'

'I had not then locked the doors,' said the Chinaman. 'I have now pressed a button, and the locks are quite, quite safe.'

'Well, keep off the Sanderson touch,' snapped Chamberlain. 'A tramp died, not him. We've ditched his Rolls where it won't be found for a long time, if it's found at all—he's just disappeared, with the girl.'

'It is your business, not mine,' said Hi Ling offhandedly, 'what you do with the girl—I, I think more of Rollison. It is quite sure now that Dougall and I will have to handle him, do not worry on that score. And now' – he shrugged – 'you will go, and we shall as always be at your service.'

Some ten minutes afterwards, Mr. Arnold Chamberlain left the 'Steam Packet'. In the interval between that and the Toff's disappearance the Toff had performed a quick-change act in a room of a friend nearby – the Toff had friends in most places – and appeared in the saloon bar of the 'Steam Packet'. The difference between the saloon bar and the four-ale was negligible – class distinction did not operate in that part of Aldgate.

The Toff was mufflered, wore a peak cap, a dirty shirt, down-at-heel shoes, and a suit that had seen many better days. He had also made minor alterations to his face with greasepaint, and he looked not unlike a stevedore who had been working in the hold of a coal-steamer. He had the swagger of the East Ender, one hand in his pocket and the other swinging at his side.

Tommy the barman, still jittery after the card incident, served him with half a pint and was surly. Rollison commented on the fact, and allowed it to be known be was out of a job.

'Well, this ain't no hemployment hexchange,' growled Tommy. '*And* you can't put nuthin' on the slate.'

'I'd like to rub your nose on the ruddy floor,' snarled the Toff. He retired with his glass to a far corner – a corner from which he could see both outside and inside, for it was close to the window – and sipped his beer.

He had plenty to think about.

The grey-haired man, as far as he knew, was a stranger in the affair – a stranger to him, that was. The description and photograph that he had of Chamberlain was entirely different from the man who had been with Hi Ling and Dougall, and there was not the slightest reason why he should associate them. But: He had contrived to frighten the trio.

And the grey-haired man knew Chamberlain.

He was in no two minds about the likely result of his interview. Hi Ling would not take the insult lying down, and Dougall was the type who would take some restraining. He realised that they would come for him, and quickly – it behoved him to be very careful. Up to a point they were unknown qualities, although he held no illusions about their dangerousness.

But – they were hired men.

So much was obvious, and he had to decide who had hired them.

He was reflecting thus when the swing-doors of the saloon bar opened and a young man entered.

There was one thing about him that engaged the Toff's interest immediately: he was well-dressed, and his clothes had come not far from Savile Row. A pleasant-looking but also angry-looking youth, and right out of place in the 'Steam Packet'.

His eyes were bright as though with anger, and his lips were tightly set. He ordered a beer and drank it down at a stretch, then glared about him.

'Gentleman spoiling for a fight,' murmured the Toff to himself, 'and he's looking for it in the right place; he wouldn't be popular here. Odd business.'

It was odd, and it attracted the Toff's immediate interest although there was not the slightest reason for him to consider the youth concerned with the trio upstairs. Another beer went the way of the first, and as the newcomer put his glass down on the bar the door opened and a second man came through.

He was under-sized, amply pock-marked, and not a creature to trust. And: 'Possessed of a squint,' said the Toff *sotto voce.*

He was alert on the instant. Here was a little man with a squint, and on the previous day he had heard of such a man who had followed him from Chamberlain's Oxford Street establishment. Squinting was no man's copyright, but at least it rang a bell of warning.

The little man stood at the door, surveying the dozen loungers with some truculence. He saw the well-dressed youth, whose back was towards him, and moving so quickly that even the Toff was surprised, he reached the other's side. His voice was illiterate but pitched low, and the Toff only just caught his words.

'I told you to git art of 'ere an' keep art. 'Ow many more times d'yer want tellin'?'

The youngster turned quickly, making no effort to keep his voice low nor to conceal his anger.

'Keep your hands off me or I'll break your blasted neck!'

He looked capable of doing it as the man with the squint swore. Two large roughnecks leaning against the bar took little interest, and Tommy the barman ignored the quarrel. Squint-Eye was well known at the 'Steam Packet', thought the Toff, and his interest quickened.

'You'd do what?' Squint-Eye's voice rose. 'You ain't wanted rahnd 'ere, if—'

The youngster acted with a speed and effectiveness which earned the Toff's approval, even though it was unwise. He grabbed his glass of beer and flung the dregs into Squint-Eye's face. The little man staggered back, taken completely by surprise. There was an ugly murmur from the two roughnecks, while two others, anticipating a rough-house, went out of the bar with celerity. The youngster faced those remaining with a spirit also earning the Toff's admiration.

'If you want trouble, I'm ready for it, I—'

The words had hardly left his mouth when the two men rushed at him. There was a sudden scurry, an oath that was not nice, and one of the toughs staggered back, blood streaming from his nose. The second gasped as suddenly and doubled up with pain from a stomach-punch, while the well-dressed youth glared round at the remaining occupants – including the Toff and Tommy – as though prepared for a concerted rush.

'The next one'll get *hurt*. Who's for it?'

Silently the Toff applauded. The voice, he fancied, was more Canadian than English, but the pugnacious one was certainly not from the United States.

There was a momentary lull.

One roughneck was still groaning, but the other was preparing for a second rush. The youngster decided to take the offensive and stepped towards him; at which moment the barman snatched a bottle from beneath the bar.

The youth's fist shot out, but his opponent was prepared this time and side-stepped. The youth went past him, carried by the force of his blow, and the barman's hand was raised with the bottle poised. The lough feinted with his right, and then let fly with his hobnailed boot for the attacker's knee. Luck saved him from the kick, but it needed more than luck to save him from the bottle.

The Toff, until that moment an apparently startled spectator, picked up an empty glass and threw it into the barman's face. It struck the man's nose, bottom first, and he gasped with pain, letting the bottle thud on to the floor.

Squint-Eye, one hand in his pocket, swung round towards the interrupter.

'You keep out o' this!'

The Toff saw him slide from his pocket something which gleamed very bright. Squint-Eye was near the impetuous stranger, who was mixing it good and proper with the only other one of his adversaries in action – he seemed more intent on any old fight than in forcing his quarrel with Squint-Eye to a conclusion. Squint-Eye went forward, apparently considering the man in the corner satisfactorily dealt with, and in his hand was a knife.

'You dirty sticker!' growled the Toff. He was a picture of an honest but outraged English working-man, his voice quivering with indignation. 'Drop it, or I'll break yer ruddy neck ...'

As he spoke he moved forward, gripping the man's knife arm in a half-nelson. Squint-Eye swore with sudden pain, and the knife clattered to the floor. The Toff stamped his heel on the blade, snapping it in two, and tightened his hold on the man who might know Chamberlain.

And then a door leading from the back of the room burst open.

The Toff saw the gigantic figure of Dougall and the impassive face of Hi Ling. Just then the Toff had no desire to try conclusions with them, and he badly wanted to talk with the hot-headed youth. In that rough-house nothing could be guaranteed, and he did not want it known that the Toff was there.

Sweat was beading Squint-Eye's forehead, for the Toff was forcing him towards the bar, maintaining his hold. They reached the struggling couple near the bar, and with his free right hand the Toff swung a pile-driver into the rough's neck. The man fell back beneath this fresh attack with the youth still clinging to him.

The Toff dropped Squint-Eye's arm but, before the man could dart away, grabbed him by the neck and ankles. He swung him twice, rejoicing in the ease of it, but maintaining his poise of outraged sense of what was done.

'I'll teach yer to use a knife, yer little swipe!'

With the 'swipe' he flung the little man bodily towards the advancing negro and Chinaman. Squint-Eye's head caught the black man in the stomach and Dougall shouted and fell back, forcing Hi Ling against the wall. Dougall's stomach was not having a nice night.

For a split second the Toff was close to the youth, who was still ready for the fight and apparently annoyed that no one else was waiting.

'Run for it,' whispered the Toff. 'They're all armed and we can't last any longer. Aldgate Pump in an hour's time. Got that?'

The youth hesitated, and for a fraction of a second seemed about to refuse. Then he saw the grey eyes of the man who was dressed like an out-of-work stevedore, and something in those eyes made him change his mind.

'Aldgate Pump it is.'

Together they moved for the door. Rollison reached it a foot ahead of one of the bruisers, who had recovered enough to want his own back, and sent the man sprawling with a short-arm jab to the jaw. He opened the door and the youngster slipped out as Hi Ling recovered from Nigger's fall.

The Toff followed, and then began to run, wondering whether the men at the 'Steam Packet' would try any funny business outside.

The door opened behind him. He heard a bottle crash on to the pavement at his side, and heard the heavy thud of footsteps. Immediately outside the 'Steam Packet' the Streets were ill lit, and he knew that many grim things could happen.

He could hear the youngster's footsteps, ten yards or so ahead of him. They paused, and he caught up with the stranger as a second bottle broke against the wall of the house where they were standing.

'Run for it,' snapped the Toff; 'I'm all right.'

'But—'

'To hell with buts, I can dodge them. Get going, and take the second right, it'll bring you to the High Street.'

There was little or no lighting even where he was, but he contrived to impress the other, who took to his heels and showed a nice turn of speed. From behind them – they had paused only for a moment – the heavy tread of at least three men was nearer. The Toff cut across the road to make sure the youngster was not followed, and looked over his shoulder. Against the light coming from the 'Steam Packet' he saw the two roughnecks and the man with the squint. Neither Dougall nor Hi Ling were taking part in the chase.

Rollison reached the other side of the road.

They were half-way across by the time he reached an alley that ran alongside warehouses towering towards the star-decked sky. He went into it, and then waited. The men came up, one muttering: 'Darn Baker's Lane—'

He turned into the alley, leading the way – and the Toff's leg shot out, tripping him up. A second followed before the warning cry reached him. Two roughnecks, unaccustomed to such cavalier treatment, sprawled into each other, while the man with the squint suddenly found himself gripped by a pair of hands that threatened to squeeze the life out of him.

The Toff had a clear plan of action in mind.

If this was the same man with the squint, Bill of Putney would identify him – and help to make him talk. It was worth the effort to get him away, and there were friends enough at hand to look after him for an hour or two.

He used a cosh to knock the man out.

Squint-Eye grunted, and dropped. The Toff turned to keep the others busy for a moment, rightly unworried by the opposition they were likely to offer, when a shrill whistle sounded above the heavy breathing.

The police!

He stopped, and stepped into the wider thoroughfare.

From two directions policemen were coming at the double, and one man's whistle was still blasting. There was no chance at all of getting away with Squint-Eye.

Rollison returned to the shadows of the alley.

'The cops,' he snapped. 'Scram!'

His attackers were united with him against the common enemy. They swung round, racing along the alley, while the Toff followed at a more leisurely gait. Twenty yards along he found what he wanted – a lower stretch of wall, surrounding the yard of a warehouse. He jumped for it, found purchase with his hands, and swung himself up. In the shadows he could see the police turning into the alley, one of them bending over Squint-Eye's outstretched form. In something under twenty seconds one Robert had hurried beneath the Toff, who then dropped to the other side of the wall and by devious ways crossed the courtyard and reached Aldgate High Street.

In five minutes he was entering a small house, one of a long, begrimed row of terraced workmen's homes. A dim gaslight showed at the end of the narrow passage, and a wireless blared forth, more tinny than most and giving evidence of old age.

A middle-aged woman was sitting at a scrubbed kitchen table, darning socks, and a young couple were sitting in close proximity on a couch from which the hair stuffing, in places, was protruding. All of them jumped.

'Well, bless *me,*' exclaimed the woman, 'if it ain't the Torf!'

He had pushed back his cap and his face was visible, but her immediate recognition gave her credit. The couple were on their feet, too startled to be annoyed at the abrupt interruption.

'Always around,' smiled Rollison. 'Ma, my clothes are over at Danny Slow's, and I don't want to go back there, a policeman might recognise me. Get them, will you?'

'Ernie'll go,' decided Ma, rising and revealing a stoutly corsetted torso mostly covered by a long, blue knitted cardigan, despite the warmth of the June evening. 'Aggie, make a cupper tea, an' look sharp about it.'

Ernie grinned and slipped out for the clothes which the Toff had changed for those of his second visit to the 'Steam Packet', Aggie – pretty in a tinsel fashion and with a light summer frock, hennaed and permanently waved hair, and reddened lips that were startlingly out of place in the small kitchen – went into the scullery to make tea. Ma sat down again and proceeded with her darning.

There was a husband, at that moment in gaol, but there on a short sentence when – but for the Toff's intervention – he might have been up for a stretch. A cheerful, happy-go-lucky soul who had meant no serious harm and, if Ma had her way, would go straight in future. By such contacts the Toff endeared himself to the majority of those who lived East of Aldgate Pump.

'I never noo you was workin',' Ma said.

'I was somewhat surprised myself,' admitted the Toff. 'Heard from Sam lately?'

''Im? *'E* won't write, 'e's too lazy to lick the pencil. After anyone?'

'Curiosity mustn't kill the cats,' said Rollison, sprawling back in the remnants of an easy chair, and as much at home here as he had been at his flat. 'Any rumours of snow, Ma?'

'There's allus too much o' that filthy stuff around. But I ain't heard nuthin' special. After some, are you?'

'I'm hoping to find it,' admitted the Toff. 'Keep your ears open, will you? Ah—Aggie, as always beautiful, and the best maker of tea in Aldgate!' He smiled at the girl, who preened herself.

The Toff drank hot and nearly black tea, to be joined shortly by Ernie, with his clothes. Fifteen minutes later, as the Hon. Richard Rollison, he took his leave after shaking hands all round. No money passed, for Ma would have been more hurt than offended at the suggestion of reward.

And she, like Bill of Putney, would keep her ear to the ground.

Chapter Nine

Frank Brendon

Some minutes after eleven o'clock a taxi drew up alongside Aldgate Pump, that landmark separating East from West in the sprawling metropolis which – the Toff was apt to say – had started from wattle huts but had not necessarily improved except in appearance, and the cabby descended and approached a square-shouldered, frowning young man who looked older than he had done in the 'Steam Packet'.

He had washed and straightened his clothes, but could do nothing to hide an embryo black eye, nor a scratch on his upper lip at which he dabbed occasionally with a handkerchief. He was fair, brown-skinned from an out-of-door life, and his general bearing impressed the Toff favourably. He stood under a street lamp, and started when the cabby reached him.

'Gennulman asked me to 'and yer this, sir.'

'This' was an unsealed envelope and the youngster glanced towards the cab before he opened it. Then he erinned, another thing that favourably impressed the Toff.

The note read:

I'm in the cab. Better meet me here. 'Steam Packet'.

He pushed the note into his pocket and followed the cabby to the taxi. Rollison opened the door and the youngster stepped in, at first seeing little, for the interior of the cab was dark.

'Regulation C—never enter a cab without seeing who's in it first,' said the Toff gently.

The other stopped short, and stared at the Toff's corner. He was sent off his balance as the cab started, steadied himself and, as the light shone into the interior, stared in unaffected astonishment.

'Who the blazes are you?'

'Same man, different trousers,' said the Toff.

'I don't believe—'

'Oh, come,' said the Toff, offering cigarettes as the other sat gingerly in the opposite corner. 'It only needed a quick change, and the voice should make you know it's the only difference.'

'Too right it should,' said the other with a quick grin. 'But when you say quick change you mean it. Did you get away all right?'

'It looks like it.'

'Yes, but I mean without any bother.'

'None to worry about,' said Rollison easily. 'You haven't done so badly, but I suppose you managed a wash-and-brush-up at the station. Fed lately?'

'Well, no—'

'Chiro's can feed a hungry man,' the Toff assured him, 'and afford us some kind of privacy. But I hope you won't be as abrupt with the customer at the next table as you were with our man with the squint. You could get thrown out properly there.'

A quick, cheerful grin greeted the sally.

'Oh, I can behave myself, but I didn't like that little runt, and—look here, who are you?'

'That can wait,' said Rollison. 'Are you sure you weren't followed?'

'Not much doubt about that; no one threw anything for a long time.'

The Toff chuckled, but watched through the rear window, making sure that there was no other cab or private car on their heels. Satisfied, he sat back and deliberately avoided conversation. He wanted to judge the stranger, and a man's reaction to silence when he was bursting to talk was one of the surer signs of reliability or otherwise. His companion smoked and made no attempt at breaking the silence, although he glanced at the Toff several times and grinned.

The square line of his jaw suggested obstinacy, and his eyes suggested a quick temper, although his manner now created the impression that he could hold temper as well as curiosity in check. Adding to the boyishness of his appearance were a number of freckles on his cheeks and at his chin.

Chiro's, off Shaftesbury Avenue, was a cross between a night-club and a restaurant, with the amenities of the former, to those who were well-liked, and the prices of the latter. Merelli, the head waiter, ushered them to a table which the Toff demanded to be secluded, and asked solicitously about the Toff's health, while boasting of Chiro's cellar. He took the order and disappeared, and it was after a grilled sole had made its appearance that Rollison said: 'Australian?'

'Right in one.' The other spoke quickly, glad that the silence was past. 'Have I passed your test?'

'I think you'll do,' smiled Rollison. 'But you mustn't do that kind of thing in the East End; even nice-natured people might get cross with you. You've a name, I suppose?'

'Brendon, Frank Brendon. Look here, who *are* you?'

'You can call me Rollison,' said the Toff, 'and don't believe all the rumours you hear about me, if there are any rumours. What took you to the "Steam Packet"?'

Brendon frowned.

'Well, it's a longish story, and I'm confoundedly hungry—'

He had a refreshing frankness.

'All right, half an hour won't hurt it, and we'll go to my flat.'

'Couldn't we have gone there right away?'

'We could,' said Rollison. 'I'll tell you why we didn't shortly.'

Brendon proved that his activities had not affected his appetite. Moreover, he was one of those young men who considered that food and conversation did not rightly go together.

Anyone who could lose his temper as he had done in the 'Steam Packet', face difficult odds and the possibility of a knife across his throat, get out quickly when told what to do, and then within two hours sit in Chiro's and look as if he had been no further than the West End all the evening, had a quality towards which the Toff was normally sympathetic.

But Brendon had not been so outwardly contented at the 'Steam Packet' as he was now.

He was hiding the anxiety which he had shown then – and at the time the Toff had come to the conclusion that he was a much-worried man.

With coffee, Rollison said: 'No longer worried, Brendon?'

The youngster eyed him squarely, and there was no suggestion of a smile on his lips.

'Like hell I'm worried, but things have altered. I was coasting around on my own, and—well, that dump down East isn't anybody's home ground. If you've ever banged your head against a brick wall you'll know what I was feeling like.' Now that the moment had come to start talking, Brendon did so quickly and without any apparent diffidence. 'I've been absolutely up against it, Rollison; I haven't known whether I was on my head or my heels. I was ripe for a scrap with anyone, and that slimy little beast with the squint had already annoyed me more than once.'

'When?' asked Rollison.

'Well—last night, and earlier this evening. Whether he just didn't like my face, I don't know. I didn't realise,' added Brendon soberly, 'that it would turn out quite such a shindy. Do knives often fly about that way in London?'

'Often enough,' said the Toff. 'But always with a purpose. Why should anyone want to kill you?'

Brendon stared.

'Was—was that their game?'

'They don't use knives for petting parties,' said the Toff. 'Squint-Eye wanted you riled, so that he could have an excuse for going for you completely. If the worst had come to the worst it would have been put down to a pub-brawl, and Squint-Eye would have been covered by his friends; there would have been no evidence for the police.'

Brendon puckered his lips.

'I didn't quite realise—I say, you took a hell of a chance.'

'I know the habits, and forewarned is thrice-armed. We will repeat the first question—why should anyone want you dead?'

'I'm damned if I know.'

Rollison shrugged.

'I hope you're not going to try giving me half a story,' he said gently. 'It won't help, and eventually it'll land you in trouble as well as me. But you still haven't explained why you're less worried now than you were.'

Brendon smiled.

'Isn't it obvious? You certainly know how to handle those people, and I knew you'd be further interested in me, I had a feeling,' he added, and he was serious again, while the Toff believed what he was saying, 'that I could rely on you.'

'You can,' said Rollison, 'as soon as I'm sure I can rely on you.'

Brendon shrugged.

'You won't take much convincing, I hope. But are we going to stay here, or can we go to your flat?'

'We can,' said Rollison, 'and we will.'

In five minutes they were outside Chiro's and stepping into a taxi. The Toff watched carefully as they started for Gresham Terrace, but he was satisfied that they were not followed. Brendon saw where he was looking and commented: 'They'd hardly be watching this place for you, would they?'

'They do so many things you wouldn't expect,' said Rollison, 'and, like the Boy Scouts, I always try to be prepared. If my man and yours are the same, they're tough customers, and well-trained in this business. I'm not unknown, and the fact that I was at Chiro's would quickly get round. That we're not followed doesn't mean it's not known—it only suggests that they've been worried enough for the time being.'

'After tonight, I should think so!'

Rollison chuckled.

'You only saw half of tonight. Anyhow …'

He did not talk seriously until they were in the flat, and Jolly had suggested sandwiches. Jolly was not abashed when the Toff told him it was too late, and suggested that he went for a walk for the sake of his health. The flat door closed, and Brendon frowned.

'Why did you send him out?'

'A walk for the sake of Jolly's health means that I want him to keep his eyes open outside,' said the Toff. 'All part of the Rollison service! I hope I've convinced you that this business is as serious as it's dangerous.'

'You have,' said Brendon, sitting back in an easy chair. 'Well—my story first?'

'Quite definitely first,' said Rollison.

'Right.' Brendon's expression hardened. 'I warn you it's a longish one, and in parts it won't make sense, but there it is. I did think once or twice that I was making a mountain out of a molehill, but now—'

'Get the preamble finished,' said the Toff, 'and come to the horses. I may be able to help you.' He knew that Brendon was trying to marshal his thoughts in order to put the story most strongly, and from that he judged that there was little in the way of facts that the youngster could present. 'Does a Mr. Arnold Chamberlain come into this business anywhere?'

Brendon looked startled.

'How the devil did you know that?'

'Not guesswork,' said Rollison comfortably. He was satisfied now that Squint-Eye was the man who had called at the Putney garage, and he had confirmed that Brendon had been to the 'Steam Packet' on an errand similar to his own, if less clearly defined. 'All right, go on.'

'It's so damned difficult to make any sense of it,' said Brendon almost irritably. 'Look here, Rollison, I'm kind of half-engaged—that is to say I will be, I hope, fairly soon. I came over from Australia a month after my—er—'

'Girl-friend,' smiled the Toff.

'Surely, girl-friend. I couldn't travel on the same ship, unfortunately, and she and her father were anxious to get here for the summer. The last I heard from Sylvia they were thinking of moving into a furnished fiat while looking round for a country house. They'd been recommended to a flat, apparently, by a man James Sanderson had met over here.'

'James Sanderson being ...?'

'Sylvia's father, of course.'

'I'd gathered that, but what does he do for a living?'

'Oh, he's a big timber merchant in Sydney, and he runs a small Australasian shipping line. Quite wealthy,' Brendon went on. 'He used to do a lot of sheep-farming, and he still has interests in some big ranches. I suppose you'd almost call him a stock-rearer made good.'

'I've got the general outline. Well, this flat, or the man who recommended it?'

'Sylvia wrote to me only ten days ago—I got the letter when we called at Marseilles. She wasn't too happy about moving to the flat, for two reasons. She was anxious to find a place in the country, and she didn't like Chamberlain—Arnold Chamberlain—who recommended it. What *do* you know about him, Rollison?'

'Not enough, but I will,' said the Toff softly. 'Go on.'

'The situation was more or less in abeyance,' said Brendon. 'There was some talk about the country house. Sylvia thought her father knew of one, but it was all kind of vague. As a matter of fact,' Brendon went on with a burst of confidence, 'the house was probably going to be Jim's—I mean Mr. Sanderson's—wedding present to us, so naturally we were more concerned with the house than anything else. But I'm still going round in circles. This is the point, Rollison: I reached here a week ago, but I couldn't get immediately to London, and when I phoned the New Piccadilly, Sylvia wasn't in.'

'Staying at the New Piccadilly, were they?' Rollison made it a comment rather than a question, and found confirmation of the fact that Sanderson was wealthy: the New Piccadilly was not made for those with limited incomes. Behind the comment, moreover, was a thought which worried him considerably, and in his mind he knew the gist of what Brendon was going to say next.

He did.

'When eventually I got to London, they'd left the hotel—on that same morning. It was rather queer, too. They'd not taken their baggage, but had sent a man and a car for it, together with the money to pay their bill. The reception clerk at the hotel didn't seem to remember much, and the manager wasn't very helpful—I just got the bare details.'

'And you haven't located them?'

'I can't find any sign of them at all,' Brendon said, and now he made no effort to repress his anxiety. 'Damn it, Sylvia wouldn't be likely to run out on me like that, I'm sure she wouldn't. Anyhow, I had only one name to work on—Chamberlain.'

'What do you know about him?'

'Well, apparently he was a fur importer,' Brendon said. 'Sylvia had persuaded a fur cape out of her father, and she mentioned it. So I was able to find the right man and went to see him. He was all right—smooth, though—as far as it went. He said he didn't know them well, but had tried to help them. They'd decided not to take a house which he had recommended, apparently. Well, I couldn't call him a liar, but I wasn't happy about it.' Brendon broke off with a laugh which held little humour. I didn't think it worth going to the police, because Sylvia might have persuaded Jim to take a trip to the coast or somewhere. They might even have gone to a flat. I *was* playing with the idea of getting a private detective when—'

Brendon broke off again, and the Toff waited.

'When,' went on Brendon slowly, 'I saw that little swine with the squint, I'd seen him before hanging about the Sandersons' place in Australia. I was sure of it, and I am still.'

'It widens the issue,' Rollison said thoughtfully. 'Well?'

'I hardly needed more telling that there was something funny on the go,' went on Brendon, 'and I decided to follow Squint-Eye. That's probably why he took a dislike to me. I suppose it was crazy not to go to the police, but I felt that I'd like to try handling the job myself. I didn't want the police worrying Sylvia and her father for nothing, you see. I noticed that every time Chamberlain left Oxford Street—I hung about a bit, hoping something would turn up—the man with the squint was around.'

'Definitely a point,' said the Toff.

'Ye-es,' Brendon said, 'but not a helpful one.' He lifted his arms in a helpless gesture. 'That's about all there is to it. I followed Squint-Eye today, and twice before I went into the "Steam Packet" for a pick-me-up he'd warned me that it wasn't a healthy neighbourhood. That rather got on my raw side and I lost my temper. The rest you know. If you hadn't butted in, it seems I'd have been in Queer Street.'

The Toff nodded, thinking hard and thinking fast. He liked young Brendon, and the story seemed likely enough; too vague for a worked-up yarn. To hang about the Oxford Street shop, half hoping that his fiancée or Sanderson himself would visit the mysterious Mr. Arnold Chamberlain, was exactly what might have been expected of him.

Apart from the plausibility of the story, as such, there were other more worrying things. On the surface of it, James Sanderson and his daughter were both missing. It was possible, of course, that the girl wanted to avoid Brendon, but unless Brendon was pitching a deliberate fake, that was unlikely. And talking of a house as a probable wedding present was fairly convincing.

So that probably the Sandersons were missing.

It seemed all of London to Timbuctoo that Chamberlain knew something about their disappearance and – the Toff fought hard against his reasoning, but it persisted – if he was right, if the body had been different from that seen by the cyclist, if the hands had been mutilated in order to make the task of identification difficult, then here was a man who could fit into the circumstances. It could be a solution of the mystery of the nameless body.

Seeing the lines of anxiety beneath Brendon's eyes, and the shadows in those steady eyes, the Toff wanted to see it differently, but he could not. It was more hunch than knowledge, and yet he did not believe himself wrong.

Sanderson, the Australian timber merchant in England with his daughter, had been murdered. Why? And why the trick with the body?

Brendon broke the silence which had lasted for several minutes.

'What's in your mind, Rollison?'

'Many things.'

'Don't hedge, please! I can take it.'

'I can't give you any information at all,' said Rollison, 'and I'm not going to feed you on half-stories. I'd never heard of the Sandersons until you mentioned them.'

'All right.' Brendon shrugged. 'What were you doing at the "Steam Packet"?'

It was a natural and fair question, but the Toff had no intention of confiding his suspicions at that moment. If Sanderson *was* dead, what of his daughter? Young Brendon would suffer mental torture if he knew how the Toff's mind was working. As the Toff connected the murder of a tramp with the missing Australian merchant, it was advisable as well as merciful to wait for facts rather than hunches. At least for the moment.

'Well,' he said, 'I make a hobby of studying Londoners in the rough, and you won't find them rougher anywhere than in that particular pub. It's the hottest spot in the hottest corner of—'

'In other words,' said Brendon resignedly, 'you don't want to talk. Well—'

'I'll give you all the help I can,' said Rollison, 'but you'll have to take me on trust, and you'll have to do what I tell you.'

Few people saw the long, lean figure, the bronzed face, and the eyes with their steady gleam, without liking the Toff. Brendon had already made up his mind about that.

'I'm on,' he said. 'I'm no good at all on my own, anyhow.'

'You'll be a big help.' said Rollison slowly. 'We can now work from both ends. I don't think Chamberlain's a nice gent, and hope to prove it. Finding your Sylvia and her father may show me the way. At all events,' he added reflectively, 'after the show-down at the "Steam Packet" there's going to be action—and quickly.'

Chapter Ten

Attack!

Four sullen, and disgruntled men lounged in the bar of the 'Steam Packet', mostly with temporary repairs to features that had been damaged in the encounter with the Toff and young Brendon.

They were worried for two reasons.

The fight had shown them that they were facing someone who knew the methods of the East End, and they were no longer convinced that it had been a chance encounter when the lounger had come to Brendon's assistance. But the other thing was more important: Nigger Dougall and Hi Ling paid good wages but expected good work. They could not claim that their work that night had been good.

Consequently they awaited further orders with trepidation.

Four equally worried men were in the underground room, for Squint-Eye had been admitted to the counsel of the others. He was badly bruised and considerably frightened. He knew that he had escaped serious injury more by a miracle than anything else, and the moment when he had been flying through the air had been the worst experience of a not uneventful life.

Chamberlain was talking.

'Where did you first see the younger man, Jaggers?'

'He started to foller you,' said Jaggers, 'and he musta seen through the dodge at the barfs, but he lorst yer down 'ere. I told him to scram—'

'Why talk to him at all?'

Jaggers saw the expression in his employer's eyes and did not like it. There was a whine in his voice as he went on: 'He mighta' seen yer comin' away, Boss, and yer didn't want 'im squealin' around the place, did yer?'

'It wouldn't have been wise.' Chamberlain realised that his bodyguard had acted for the best. 'Young Brendon will have to go. You'll arrange it, Dougall?'

Nigger nodded, but this time he did not grin. He was still shaken – physically by the impact of Jaggers on his solar plexus, mentally by memory of the Toff's card, and the first interview.

Hi Ling, now dressed in a well-cut suit of blue serge, but contriving to look even more Oriental than before, spoke softly: 'But his fliend? The other man?'

'If I ever see 'im again,' began Jaggers viciously, 'I'll slit 'is blastid froat! I'll—'

He made a motion across his neck.

'You did not succeed with your knife tonight,' said Hi Ling softly. 'He showed so remarkable ability for a fight did that strange man.'

Dougall stared uneasily.

'What's on yuhr mind, Ling?'

'Only once,' said Hi Ling imperturbably, 'have I seen such grey eyes before. Only once, my fliend.'

'Who do you mean?' snapped Chamberlain.

'You also have seen them. Rollison—'

'It couldn't be! He hadn't left us long; his clothes—'

'I think it was the Toff,' said Hi Ling. He stared at Chamberlain, who had started to pour whisky into a tumbler. 'Rollison would change swiftly, not far from here. None other could have acted quite as he did. Do you understand now, my friend, the man against whom you would set us?'

Chamberlain tossed off his drink.

'Ye-es. If he did that he's good, but we've got to get him as well as Brendon more than ever now.'

'Why don't yuh lie low fer a bit?' asked Dougall. 'Rollison won't ease off for a while, and—'

'This isn't the time for waiting,' snapped Chamberlain. 'We can hold up the snow and the jewels, but the Sanderson job's started and it's got to be finished.'

'All things can wait,' said Hi Ling impassively.

Chamberlain's lips curled.

'If I say it's urgent, it's urgent. Maybe you want a showdown—well, here it is. I can squeal on you any time I want to, and trying funny stuff here won't help you! Break with me and you break yourselves. You're taking big money, and I've got you' – he touched the table, pressing on the ball of his thumb until the flesh was white – 'there. You'll do what I say.'

'So?' Hi Ling's voice was dangerously quiet. 'You are being foolish, mistah. Nigger and I, we are not men to be treated like dogs. Remember that, my fliend.'

For a moment there was silence, while the Chinaman's eyes met Chamberlain's, unflinching and inscrutable. The fur importer knew suddenly that he was no match for Hi Ling; he could have handled Dougall alone, but the combination was too strong. It would be his best policy to keep on their right side. The heavy hand would be dangerous.

'Surely,' he said sharply. 'I'm not aiming to pick a quarrel, Hi Ling, but I tell you that it's too dangerous to let the Toff and young Brendon alone; they know too much. It's no safer for you than for me, and if I've got to shout to make you understand, you can't blame me.'

Hi Ling shrugged.

'That is difflent,' he said; 'but' – his voice was barely above a whisper – 'should you not tell us just why we have run these risks to kill Sanderson and to take his so-beautiful daughter a prisoner?'

Chamberlain's face was taut, and the muscles beneath his eyes twitched. Only by considerable exercise of self-control did he prevent himself from swearing at the Chinaman, who had revealed himself more fully that night than ever before. Rollison and Brendon must be handled first; Hi Ling could be dealt with later.

'That's my business,' he said slowly. 'You get paid well for everything you do, but you don't get paid for asking questions.

We've got to understand each other. You're partners in other things, but in the Sanderson game you just take orders.'

Hi Ling bowed, and there was mockery in his eyes.

'A thousand pardons! We shall proceed with arrangements for the disposal of Rollison, and we will take care of Brendon. But there is another thing …'

'Well?'

'We still have the body of the tramp,' said Hi Ling gently. 'It is as well the body is removed. Velly often the interest of Rollison blings the interest of the police.'

'Tie a weight round it and dump it in the Thames,' said Chamberlain. 'There's no need to keep it any longer.'

'It will be arranged,' said Hi Ling smoothly.

The fur importer was scowling as he stood up. He had experienced the most harassing hours of his life, and he recalled with sudden vividness the fear which Dr. Vincent Lowerby had evinced of the Toff. There *was* something uncanny about the Toff …

He pushed thought of the man aside.

An hour later, after removing his grey wig, replacing his horn-rimmed glasses, and changing his clothes at the convenient Turkish baths, Chamberlain hurried to Oxford Street. Five minutes later Jaggers telephoned that no one had followed him. Chamberlain heaved a sigh of relief, then cursed himself for letting Rollison get on his nerves.

Hi Ling played no inconsiderable part in his thoughts, for now that he was away from the 'Steam Packet' he was able to view the attitude of the Chinaman more calmly. It was not a pleasant attitude. There was excuse enough for Hi Ling wanting to know about the Sanderson angle, but …

Chamberlain shrugged. Hi Ling could continue wanting.

The telephone on his desk rang sharply an hour after Chamberlain reached his office the next morning. He did not expect anything but a normal business call, and he had a jolt when he heard Jaggers' harsh voice.

'Well, what is it?'

Jaggers drew a deep breath.

'Boss, there's a coupla dicks—'

'*What?*'

'Cops—narks; I'd recognise them anywhere,' said Jaggers urgently. 'They're watching the shop, Boss; there ain't no doubt about that. Maybe they ain't watching you, but—'

'We'll try it out,' said Chamberlain.

The possibility of the need for watching the police did not worry him so much as might have been expected. The possible danger from them was known, and he also knew their methods. It was disturbing to think they were interested in him.

Twenty minutes later he went out.

In an hour he was back at the salerooms, and he knew that he had been followed on several innocent and genuine business calls. Jaggers was right, and now he had to face the police as well as Rollison and Brendon.

'Which means moving very fast,' he said slowly, as he sat back in his chair. 'If Rollison's put the police on to me—'

He shrugged. Guessing was no use, but action would be. One thing was certain: Hi Ling and Dougall had to be kept in ignorance of the police interest.

Hi Ling and Dougall had been considering their position with Arnold Chamberlain since he had left the 'Steam Packet' the previous night. They were well aware of the side on which their bread was buttered. The organization which they helped Chamberlain to control was a paying one, and, until Rollison had shown such interest, relatively safe. They had not the slightest desire to cease their co-operation with the handling of illegal drugs and the trafficking in stolen jewels. But to them it appeared that Chamberlain's personal interest in Sanderson, not the normal work, was bringing the danger from Rollison.

Had they known the whole truth of the Sanderson angle they might have been satisfied. But, apart from their ignorance, there was also the fact that they were obeying orders rather than co-operating. It displeased Hi Ling in particular.

But the issue was clear.

Rollison was the danger.

'Chamberlain's askin' fer trouble,' said Nigger Dougall, obstinately, about the time that Chamberlain was proving the interest of the police in him. 'Let him have it, Ling.'

'And to lose so much?' Hi Ling murmured.

'We got a mighty big pile—'

'It can be bigger. And' – the Chinaman's eyes were not pleasant – 'can you easily forget last night, Dougall? Does not Rollison invite much trouble?'

Dougall swore.

'If I could be sur've getting him—'

'There is, I think, a way,' said Hi Ling softly. 'Like all the good ways, it is simple, Dougall. We shall work ourselves, and not trust by themselves the fools who tried last night to get Brendon. You will listen …'

And after a while Dougall agreed to work.

At half past ten that night a closed saloon car was waiting in Gresham Street, which turns off Gresham Terrace. The uniformed chauffeur was so huddled in his coat that the fact that he was a Chinaman was not obvious.

At twenty-five minutes to eleven the Hon. Richard Rollison passed the stationary car, but did not give it more than passing thought. Large, ostentatious cars did stop in that neighbourhood at all times of the day and night; chauffeurs were often compelled to while away weary hours waiting on the whims of employers with money to burn. True, Gresham Street was a less likely place than Gresham Terrace for a luxury car – the street was not one with the best of reputations. But it was an excellent parking-place.

The Toff knew that after dark Gresham Street was haunted by shadowy figures, contriving to keep in the background and yet always obvious. And all feminine. Quick meetings, a 'Hallo, dearie!' and a couple walking hurriedly and furtively away, were commonplace.

The Toff was not thinking of that.

He had been to the New Piccadilly Hotel, and learned that James and Sylvia Sanderson had done precisely what Brendon had said. The manager had been surprised, but it was not, after all, so much out of the ordinary, and there had been no question of unpaid bills. He had given it little thought; and so had the clerk who had received the money from the messenger from Sanderson. There had been nothing remarkable about the messenger, and the Toff failed to get a worth-while description.

Another dead end.

There were far too many in this affair, but he believed that the Sanderson angle would see the end of them. He was considering the next step to take against Chamberlain when he saw a man walk quickly on the other side of the street and stop suddenly in front of a girl. A moment later the silence of the night was pierced by a high-pitched scream.

The Toff halted in his tracks and swung round. He saw the man push the girl to the pavement, and heard her screaming again, with high-pitched, terrified cries fit to waken the dead. The Toff did the only thing that there was to do. He began to run very fast.

At the moment of the scream the powerful saloon car had started to move.

Only its wing-lamps were on, and at first the engine purred softly, but as the Toff moved it roared and the car shot forward. The Toff was half-way across the road when he saw the wing-lamps growing nearer, saw the big car moving towards him. In that fraction of a second he knew that he had fallen into a trap, while eternity was yawning before him.

Chapter Eleven

Facts About Sanderson

The Toff had time neither to go back nor to go forward. Whichever way he moved there was no time to evade the onrush of the car, since the driver's one object was to run him down. He had hardly time to think, only to realise the likely end.

He felt a sudden nausea, but his face was expressionless as he moved, knowing that he had to try to escape, yet realising the weight of the odds against him. The roar of the engine was loud in his ears, and although it happened so swiftly it seemed an age from the moment that he had started to cross the road.

He did not see the girl standing up and staring now, but not screaming. Nor the man who had accosted her, farther down the street and peering along it – although, had he been able to see him, Rollison would have recognised one of the men of the 'Steam Packet'.

He did not see Hi Ling at the wheel.

The Chinaman's face was expressionless but for the glitter of triumph in his eyes. He knew Rollison had no time to judge a jump, knew that he had found a weakness where no one else had done.

The car smashed onwards.

The Toff went down.

There was another scream from someone nearby, a second, a third, and the car passed over Rollison's body without stopping, swung round into Gresham Terrace and then towards Piccadilly, slowing down as it reached the main thoroughfare and then moving more sedately towards the Circus. The number-plate was changed by automatic control, and at the wheel Hi Ling actually laughed.

The girl in Gresham Street did not laugh.

For as half a dozen people rushed towards the Toff's fallen figure it moved – and the movement was not that of a badly injured or dying man. The movement, in fact, was quick and lissome, and the Toff snapped: 'Did anyone follow that car?'

He had no answer. No one watching believed he was really on his feet; it took time to understand that a miracle had happened – or what seemed a miracle. Obviously no one had followed the car, and the Toff swore, but beneath his breath.

In a side turning the girl who had screamed almost banged into Nigger Dougall, who had been watching from a safe distance, but had not seen the miracle, since he could not see through flesh and blood.

'Nice work, Dolly, very nice work—'

'He—he ain't hurt!'

Dougall stared.

'Don't you start—Who said he wasn't?'

'I see him, didn't I? He got up, he yelled something about the car. He ain't hurt!'

'Let's get outa here,' snapped Dougall, and as he hurried towards a taxi he felt a clammy sweat at the nape of his neck, for it seemed unnatural for any man to have evaded the car, and it was said of the Toff that he was not human. Not far back there were primitive beliefs and customs in the mind of Nigger Dougall; the effect of centuries of credence in witchcraft and medicine men needed little to reassert itself. As he sat back in the cab he was muttering to himself, as if trying to find spells that would keep the Toff away from him.

While the Toff had been out Frank Brendon had been at the flat, without liking it. He found it difficult not to trust the Toff completely, but on the other hand he felt that he had to do something, and the Toff's silence, more than what he had said, worried him.

Did he know anything about Sylvia?

Brendon, not knowing that the Toff could do no more than guess, felt convinced that something was being kept back from him for the sake of his feelings. He preferred to know the worst, and he tried to get it from Jolly. Jolly was expansive – on the subject of Mr. Rollison's cricketing prowess, his habit of spending long holidays abroad, his earlier 'adventures' – Jolly used the word with a slight scorn, as if he thought another word the better in the circumstances – and his *affaires*. On his *affaires* Jolly was at once discreet, admiring and comprehensive.

Towards ten o'clock Jolly had gone out, and he had not returned when Brendon had looked out of the window and imagined he could see Rollison at the corner which turned into Gresham Street. The Toff had urged – in fact virtually commanded – him not to leave the flat, and had also talked of the murder of a tramp as his only connection – indirectly – with Arnold Chamberlain. All that had done was to increase Brendon's belief that the older man was keeping something back from him.

Then he heard the roar of the car engine.

From the height of the window he could see most of what happened, and he guessed the rest. For some seconds he stood transfixed. Then he swung round, flung open the door and rushed downstairs.

He pushed his way through the crowd, by then reinforced by two policemen also nearing Rollison. He was quite convinced he would see a mangled body; instead he heard the Toff complain that someone should have followed that car.

Brendon leaned heavily against the shoulder of a man next to him, and told himself he did not believe it. Dazedly he listened to the Toff's story to the police. The Toff, of course, claimed that he had no idea who had driven at him, and was free with his comments about drunken drivers. In five minutes the police were moving the crowd along, and Rollison came towards Brendon, his lips smiling but his eyes hard.

'Hallo, young fellow—see much of that?'

'So much that I don't believe it happened.'

'It did,' said the Toff grimly. 'And yet it didn't; but we'll have to work that one out later. I want a drink.'

'Sure you're all right, sir?' asked a constable.

'Quite, thanks.' Rollison lifted a hand, and went towards the flat, a hand on Brendon's shoulder. Ten minutes later he said cheerfully: 'All I've got to show for that is a large bump on the back of my head.'

'But how the devil did you dodge it?' demanded Brendon. 'I saw the whole thing. I could have sworn—'

'I didn't have time to dodge,' said the Toff easily. 'I dropped down between the wheels; it had a high axle. A foot swerve either way would have finished me, but a car going at that speed doesn't swerve much, and the driver preferred not to swerve, anyhow. I've been closer than that, if not much. The cunning increases.'

'The what?' Brendon looked startled. 'You don't think that's connected with—'

'Mr. Chamberlain's friends,' said the Toff cheerfully. 'I do. A nicely-put-up job, for they knew I'd jump across the road if I heard a girl shout. So they arranged for her to yell, making me turn in a direction where I couldn't see the car coming. In other words, they staged the job near the corner, to have a get-out in case the police caught them. Even if the car had stopped it would—or its driver would—have a reasonably sound excuse. Any driver might have run me down as I jumped into the road without looking either way.'

'Then how do you know it wasn't an accident?'

'Because any sane driver would have tried to slow down before reaching me, even if he panicked when he realised that he couldn't avoid me, and not drove on. Don't try to hide it, Brendon; that was one of the moves against us. And it's why I don't want you to go about by yourself. You've struck something dangerous, and you're not used to countering the moves.'

Brendon looked haggard.

'It's—damnable! And—and you think Sylvia's in the hands of those swine?'

The Toff took advantage of Jolly's unexpected entry into the room to order coffee. Then he put a hand on the younger man's shoulder.

'I don't even know where Sylvia is; except that she apparently disliked Chamberlain there's no reason for thinking she's in the affair at all. If she is you can be quite sure she's unhurt.'

'How can you know?'

The Toff shrugged.

'I'd make a guess that Sanderson would pay a lot of money to ensure Sylvia's safety.'

'He certainly would.'

'And he's a rich man.'

'He must be worth half a million, but—'

'Then I'd guess again,' said Rollison quietly and with a confidence in his tone that imparted itself to the younger man, 'that it's a simple matter of ransom. Let's suppose that Chamberlain's holding both father and daughter for a few days, and then letting the father go, having put the fear of God into him. Is Sanderson going to hesitate in paying a tidy sum to make sure his daughter's all right?'

Brendon stared.

'You really think that's the swine's game?'

'I can't think of anything more likely,' said Rollison, and although he had pitched the story on the spur of the moment, to try to get Brendon's mind off the possibility of tragedy, he almost considered it possible. 'How well do you know James Sanderson?'

'Oh, as well as anyone, I suppose. He's not easy to know, although he's as straight as they're made. A lot of men who came in from the beyond—I mean who made a pile in gold or sheep before reaching the cities—are hard to get at, you know. Sylvia was absolutely devoted to him, and that's a good enough answer for me. Jim's all right.'

It was not only faith, but it was faith with some reason, Rollison admitted.

He was feeling shaken, but on the other hand the escape had made him realise that his prophecy of likely action had been fulfilled, and that Hi Ling – obviously it was the kind of scheme to occur to the Chinaman – would not be able to work so neat a plot again. Moreover, it suggested that the motive for his quick death was urgent – and when men were working hurriedly they were liable to do strange things, including wrong ones.

That urged him to act quickly.

And it urged him to find out all he could of Sanderson.

If his presumptions were right – and so far he had no reason for believing them wrong – Sanderson and the girl had been kidnapped by Chamberlain, through Dougall and Hi Ling. Chamberlain was directing the affair, and almost certainly his was the interest in Sanderson.

It seemed an even bet that Sanderson was dead, and the body had been mutilated to prevent definite identification. And the Toff kept his mind on one unalterable fact: the face had not been touched, but the fingers had. Finger-prints were more reliable than facial characteristics.

Everything, of course, depended on the presumption that Sanderson was the murdered man, and while there was nothing else to work on, Rollison proposed to Garry the theory as far as he could. And Brendon, worried about Sylvia and jolted by the affair of the car, was more likely to give things away that night than at any Lime previously. Rollison had imagined that his 'Sylvia was devoted to him, and that's good enough for me' had been more dogmatic than wholly genuine.

If so, why?

'Is he well known in Sydney?' he asked.

'Eh—oh, Jim. Yes, you'd say he was well known. Not that he'd many friends, and he didn't conduct much business personally. But—what are you getting at, Rollison?'

'You'll see. Was he thinking of retiring?'

'Oh yes—in fact he had retired from active business, although he was going to keep a controlling interest.'

'Did you expect his retirement?'

Brendon looked thoughtful.

'Well—"expect's" rather a strong word. It *was* a bit of a surprise really, but then there's no reason at all why he shouldn't retire.'

'Nor why he should?'

'Well, no.' Brendon looked uncomfortable. 'Actually most of his branches were run by managers, and he always avoided the limelight. He worked hard, but always behind the scenes—I mean, he didn't spend all his time in an office or anything like that.'

'Any peculiarities about him?'

'Just what do you mean?'

Rollison shrugged.

'Let's be wholly frank, Brendon. From what you've said of Sanderson, you don't know him well. The impression is that he's a kind of power behind the scenes—his influence is always there but he doesn't obtrude himself. Right?'

'I suppose it is,' said Brendon uncomfortably. 'He—he would never have his photograph taken, for instance.'

'Wouldn't he, by Jove! The reason?'

'I'm blessed if I know.'

'If he'd met a party of Australians at the New Piccadilly,' went on the Toff, 'would they have recognised him? Is he a reasonably well-known figure, or does he keep in the background socially as well as commercially?'

'He does rather, yes.'

'I see.' Rollison was sitting back in an easy chair, one leg drooping over the side. His eyes were narrowed and he was smoking a cigarette with apparent enjoyment. 'On the whole, then, you'd say he was scared and hiding from something?'

Brendon started up.

'Of all the rotten things to say! Of course he wasn't—'

'This is a murderous business,' said Rollison quietly. 'I tell you that the picture you've drawn of James Sanderson is of a man who was anxious not to be known, and a man anxious not to be known usually has some reason. Right?'

Brendon glowered.

'It's all very well, but—'

'Oh, to hell with you!' snapped the Toff. 'I'm wasting my time on the affair. I can approach Chamberlain from an angle that will be easier for me, and if you're going to be obstinate I can't help you. You're not talking to the police, you know.'

'Too right I'm not! I—' Brendon stepped to the window and

stared out into the lighted street. Rollison lit another cigarette, and it was five minutes before the youngster turned. His expression was set, but not with hostility.

'Sorry, Rollison. This business has got me. I'm worried to hell about Sylvia. But Jim Sanderson was a worried man, I think. I always had that impression, and before he left Sydney Sylvia told me she thought he was. I've known them both for years—I'm in the timber business, too, although not in such a big way as Sanderson—and I've always thought Jim had a worry at the back of his mind.'

'Did any one thing make you think so?'

'Well, he always hated meeting new people. Wouldn't go to dances and balls, and that kind of thing. When he went to a theatre he booked through an agency, and—well, he always seemed anxious to keep alone. But I'm as sure as I'm standing here that he's straight,' Brendon added slowly.

'There's no reason to think differently,' said Rollison. 'I'm glad to have the yarn, Brendon; it might help. Well, try to get some sleep now. The morning'll give us a fresh start.'

Brendon went into the spare room, leaving the Toff to ponder. The sum total of it was that James Sanderson had some good reason for being afraid.

Afraid of whom?

In the Toff's mind was the name Arnold Chamberlain.

And, of course, the knowledge that Sanderson had not allowed himself to be photographed. Had the murderers known that? Was that why the face had been untouched but the hands ill-treated?

Chapter Twelve

Interview With Chamberlain

Sylvia had no idea how long she had been there.

It was the same room, and she had seen only one man, an old, wizened creature who spoke no word to her, but brought her food and drink three times each day, collecting the empty plates and crockery after an hour.

The small window allowed little light, but she was able to read – when she could bring her mind to do so – for there was ample electric light, and a small book-case had been provided containing a variety of reading. Several magazines, all old, were also in the room.

The night was the worst time.

Twice she had kept the light burning all the time, but on the third night – without realising it was the third – she had managed to sleep a little in the dark, only to awaken screaming, and with a picture of the moment when her father had been killed vivid in her mind, a nightmare that left her cold and shivering as if with ague.

No one to talk to.

No knowledge of what was going to happen.

No knowing why her father had been murdered.

Only the knowledge that he had always been afraid of something unknown, and that latterly he had seemed to grow more and more apprehensive. She believed that one of the reasons for the trip to England had been to escape the unknown.

What could it be?

Questions without answer. Dreadful memories. No one to talk to, nowhere to move but the small confines of the tiny room. There were moments when she thought she was going mad.

Into the telephone at the Ridings Sir George Mannering spoke with more vigour than he was wont to use. His cricket week, for the first time in his life, was proving a failure. One match scratched – one nearly lost – and now two without Rollison. And there was the unsolved murder of the tramp to put the final touch to his ill-temper.

Sir George did not consciously think like that.

Consciously his first anxiety was the apprehension of the murderer; and he let Dawbury realise it, as well as the Inspector who came down from Scotland Yard, but so far had failed to contribute anything useful to the investigation. From the first Mannering had believed that bringing in the Yard was unnecessary. Now he was sure; and that was Rollison's fault.

He wished Rollison to perdition.

He did not say so in so many words, but Rollison gathered their drift as he heard what Mannering did say. Half-way through he interrupted the Chief Constable, and even chuckled.

'It isn't really as bad as that, old man. *I* didn't commit your murder!'

'You're murdering my cricket week,' growled Sir George.

'You're losing your sense of proportion,' said the Toff. 'But it remains a fact that I can't come down solely to play cricket. Your murder has wider ramifications than you wot of, George.'

'Eh?'

'That's all I can tell you,' said the Toff, 'but I knew you'd be delighted to know that I'm not idle. Things are happening. I rang to make sure that you've nothing new your end.'

'We haven't a thing,' confessed Mannering, and then slyly: 'Except more confirmation that the dead man was a tramp. Two or three villagers reckon that they recognise him as a man who was walking through a village near here last week.'

'I hope they're prepared to read their Bible before they swear on it,' said Rollison. 'Good luck for today's match.'

'A lot you care,' retorted Mannering.

He wanted to ask several questions, but Rollison had rung down before the opportunity presented itself. Mannering turned round. Entering the room was his butler.

'Yes, Adams?'

'There's a Mr. Meer to see you, sir.' Adams contrived to say "Mr. Meer" in a way that conveyed Meer's association with commerce. An antique dealer was no higher in Adams's estimation than a butcher or grocer, and a gentle, white-haired, benevolent antique dealer remained just a shopkeeper.

'Meer, Meer? Oh yes, the man from Hersham. What does he want?'

'He refused to say, sir.'

'Oh. All right, I'll see him.'

Mannering, who despite his activities with the Surrey Constabulary contrived to interest himself in most of the local charitable organizations, knew Augustus Meer as a generous contributor to many of them. A shy, retiring man, and one who gave the impression of good breeding.

Mr. Meer entered, inclined his head and offered his hand. Mannering shook it, and indicated a chair.

'Sit down, Mr. Meer. Will you smoke?'

'Thank you, no. I indulge rarely—very rarely.' Meer's expression was not unlike it had been on the occasions when he had approached Simonson of the National Bank for an extension of his overdraft. Mannering was afraid that a request for some kind of assistance was coming, and unconsciously stiffened his attitude.

'What can I do for you?'

'I'm a little vague,' smiled Mr. Meer, as if that was so rare a thing that it puzzled him. 'I'm by no means sure that I should come to you, Sir George, but—it's most worrying, most worrying indeed.'

'If you'll tell me what it is I may be able to help,' said Mannering.

'Of course, of course. I—perhaps I should have gone to the police-station, but, frankly, Sir George, I much prefer to deal with—er—with you than your excellent Inspector. I have been most distressed by the death of that poor, poor fellow—the tramp, Sir George.'

'Yes, most distressing, but—'

'I think—I think I ought to tell you,' said Mr. Meer, 'that I took one of my rare, very rare walks on the morning of the murder. I am rather a cricketer, you know—in my humble armchair fashion.' Sir George warmed to the man. 'I walked out to see the first match here—a wonderful innings by Mr. Rollison; I—'

For perhaps the first time in his life Mannering was less interested in cricket than in another subject. The possibility that, in his quiet, sleepy fashion, Meer had seen something that might be of service made him speak with more abruptness than was his wont.

'Yes, yes; but what did you see, Mr. Meer?'

The weak eyes behind the strong glasses blinked.

'I hope, I do hope I am not saying something to injure an innocent person, Sir George, but in the field—the field where the—er—body was found—I saw a man, an unusual man for this part of England. I—' Mr. Meer leaned forward, one hand lifted as if to prepare the other for the sensation – 'A full-blooded negro, Sir George!'

Mannering sat back quickly in his chair and did not even try to hide his disappointment.

'Oh yes, we've heard about him. You didn't see a Chinaman too, did you?'

'A—what? I beg your pardon, but—'

'Sorry,' rumbled Sir George. 'It seems that a negro and a Chinaman are connected with this business, Mr. Meer, but I'm afraid we haven't traced them yet, nor have we made much progress. I was hoping that you would mention something fresh.'

Mr. Meer looked his distress.

'I am so sorry, so very sorry, to have raised your hopes unwittingly. I have thought this matter over so much since the unhappy news reached me, and I felt bound—' Meer stood up, taking his glasses off for a moment and replacing them, to stare mildly at the Chief Constable – 'I felt bound to report it, although I must confess that I feel glad that, even indirectly, I have not brought information that might lead a man to the gallows.'

Mannering shrugged his shoulders.

'Whoever killed the tramp deserves hanging, Mr. Meer. Hmm. Very good of you to come along.'

'Oh, not at all, not at all. I'm going to watch the game for a few hours; such a delightful spot for cricket. I have always admired your pitch, and the setting—your efforts for the great game have such a beneficial effect on the surrounding neighbourhood, Sir George.'

Mannering thawed.

'Glad you like it,' he smiled. 'I *am* proud of the pitch; there's not a finer one in the country in its purely natural state. And a lot of runs have been knocked up here.'

'Indeed yes. I like to watch from the copse of oaks,' said Meer, revealing the enthusiasm only a cricketer shows, 'where I can follow the flight of the ball so well. I must say that Mr. Rollison's innings on Monday was a delight, a positive delight. Dare I hope he is playing today?'

I'm afraid not,' said Mannering. 'He's busy in London, I think.'

'Dear me! So unfortunate when the claims of business prevent one from following one's heart's desire.'

'Hardly business,' chuckled Mannering. 'Mr. Rollison is well known in another sphere, although you would hardly know that. He is a clever criminologist, Mr. Meer.'

'A—criminologist? Mr. *Rollison!* You astound me—astound me!' exclaimed Meer. 'Of all the unexpected things, I—but then, you are what one might also term a criminologist,' he added, 'and also a very useful cricketer. Obviously the two occupations *can* run side by side.' He smiled in gentle congratulation. 'Well, Sir George, I appreciate the kindliness with which you have listened to my somewhat belated story. I hope, I do hope, I shall not have to give evidence, but if duty demands it of me—'

'I'll see that it's avoided, if possible,' said Mannering heartily, knowing Meer would make a bad witness. A chiming of a hall clock told him that he would soon have to change into flannels, and he wanted to be rid of the dealer.

Meer wandered slowly towards the cricket field.

A handful of the older folk from nearby villages had already gathered beneath the spreading branches of the oaks which made up Meer's favourite corner. Several people from Hersham had also arrived, and many a cap was doffed as Mr. Meer passed.

The visitors batted, and their batting lacked enterprise – so much so that just before lunch Mr. Meer stood up from his seat and walked slowly towards the gates leading to the Hersham road.

He was half-way to the town when a car pulled up alongside him. Glancing up in surprise, Meer saw the heavy, reddened features of Dr. Lowerby.

'Why, Doctor, good morning—'

'This is more like,' said Lowerby heartily. 'Better than staying in bed all day. Care for a lift?'

'That is most kind of you, thank you.' Meer stepped into the car, and was soon discussing antiques. He had had few new pieces in since Lowerby had bought the Chippendale cabinet, but a small Sheraton table might be of interest to the doctor. Mr. Meer waxed enthusiastic about the Sheraton table, and Lowerby wondered whether it would be a good piece for buying and selling at a profit to Chamberlain.

He examined it, just inside the dusty, darkened interior of the shop, and asked the price.

'Well—it's so difficult to assess values,' said Meer. 'I paid—let me see—well, supposing we say thirty-five pounds, Doctor? I can't *guarantee* its genuineness, but if I have made a mistake I shall be only too glad to buy it back from you at the same figure.'

Lowerby pursed his lips.

'Thirty-five—well, it's higher than I wanted at the moment. I might manage thirty—'

'I can hardly refuse to meet you,' said Meer. 'Thirty pounds it is, Doctor. Are you going straight home, or—'

'Yes, I'll take it with me,' said Lowerby.

He put it in the back of his Morris, chattered for a few minutes to Meer, the while he decided to try a three-figure price on Chamberlain. Lowerby, who was receiving regular supplies of drugs, was also finding life very satisfactory; and it amazed him now that he should ever have been so frightened of Chamberlain, particularly when the man continually bought 'antiques' from him at prices so far above their value.

Meer waited in the doorway of his shop and watched the car disappear. Then he turned back into the gloom, while from the other side of the road a man of medium height, dressed in black, and with a dyspeptic expression on his pale face, showed a surprising interest in an off-licence until both Lowerby and Meer were out of sight.

Immediately he turned to a telephone kiosk and put through a call to London.

'Yes, Jolly?' responded the Toff amiably.

'You might be interested to hear, sir, that Dr. Lowerby has purchased a faked' – Jolly uttered the 'faked' with superb contempt – 'Sheraton table from a Mr. Meer, and has taken it home with him.'

'Yes?' said the Toff. 'I once bought a faked assegai and brought it home. I was very young at the time, but—'

'You believed it genuine, sir, and you bought it because of your interest in weapons. Dr. Lowerby, sir, is not interested in antiques. At least, there are none visible from any of the downstairs windows of his house.'

'A point,' said the Toff slowly. 'Follow Lowerby, Jolly.'

'Very good, sir.'

At the Gresham Terrace flat Rollison turned to Brendon, who was sitting near him. Brendon knew that Jolly had left early that morning for an unknown destination, and realised it was in connection with the quest for proof of Chamberlain's illegal activities. He showed a praiseworthy restraint, and to reward him the Toff gave him a brief resume of Lowerby's part – as far as it was known – in the affair.

'It's all bits and pieces,' Brendon said irritably.

'Yes, of course,' said Rollison. 'Our job's to fit the bits into the pieces. And eventually we will. Sylvia didn't give you any particulars of this house, did she?'

'No—it was only being vaguely talked about.'

'No district?'

'No. What's in your mind?'

'They might have left the New Piccadilly to look for the house,' said Rollison. 'But as Chamberlain is probably the only one who knows which house it was, that doesn't help much.'

'Nothing helps much,' said Brendon dispiritedly.

'You'd be surprised,' Rollison said.

He did not add that it seemed at least possible that the house – if the Sandersons had gone to look at one – would be somewhere near Hersham. To have intimated that would have been associating the disappearance of Bren-don's friends too clearly with the murder. He thought it, none the less.

And he had a keen desire to talk with Arnold Chamberlain.

Putting his head into the lion's den was an occupation at which the Toff showed to advantage. Nothing, he claimed, was dangerous if it were done openly. He telephoned the Oxford Street showrooms, to learn that Chamberlain was out, but was expected that afternoon soon after four o'clock.

Rollison gave his name and promised to call at four-thirty.

That at least would give Chamberlain an opportunity for avoiding the meeting if he wanted to. Also it gave the Toff time to slip to the East End and to visit several friends, including the woman who had offered him hospitality on the night of the 'Steam Packet' fracas.

His quest was simple: he wanted to find if there was much traffic reported in 'snow' – the vernacular for cocaine.

There was no unusual activity, as far as he was able to discover, but there were rumours that there was a lot of the stuff about. He could get no further than that, and he turned his questions to the recent open activities of Dougall and Hi Ling. That odd association of aliens was known but not liked by some East Londoners, but reluctantly the several whom Rollison questioned were compelled to admit there were no outward signs of illegal activity.

The small cargo boats – little more than coast craft, although they travelled frequently to and from Holland, France and Belgium – which Hi Ling owned were doing their normal trading, although neither the negro nor the Chinaman had been seen in person for some days. For that matter, they always kept in the background; few people knew them as the Controllers of the shipping line.

Rollison wrinkled his forehead.

There was a distinct possibility that through the shipping end of the business he would learn something useful about Hi Ling. And at the back of his mind was the uncomfortable thought that in Australia James Sanderson ran several ships, mostly for coastal work.

'There could be a connection,' admitted the Toff. 'We'll see whether Uncle Arnold will talk about it.'

Chamberlain – not wholly to the Toff's surprise-received him precisely at four-thirty.

The big, squarely built American, with the clean-shaven face, luxuriant black hair, and the thick horn-rimmed glasses, sat back in his swivel chair and eyed Rollison keenly, if warily. He looked what he made himself out to be – the Big Business man with no time to waste.

'Well, Rollison, what's on your mind?'

'You,' said the Toff, and had an irritating feeling that he had seen the man before. He pushed that aside as he tapped a cigarette on his thumb-nail. 'We needn't beat about the bush, need we?'

'I'm not beating anything.'

'Unless it's the law,' said the Toff gently. 'But we won't go into that. The real purpose of my visit, one might say, is to try to find a really charming country house—'

The words came so casually that he was able to study their effect on Chamberlain thoroughly. He saw the man's start of surprise, he saw Chamberlain put both clenched fists on the table – and he remembered that the grey-haired man at the 'Steam Packet' had done exactly the same thing.

That had been Chamberlain!

He had no doubt in his mind, and the discovery gave him deep satisfaction after the first surprise – but no more than the fact that Chamberlain was startled out of his equanimity by the mention of a country house.

For that, to say the least, was interesting. Brendon certainly would have jumped to conclusions.

Chapter Thirteen

Shock For Brendon

The Toff would have been the first to acknowledge that there was nothing normal or straightforward about the murder of the tramp – assuming it had been a tramp – and the case which followed it. The development which had come through Brendon had done nothing to make the affair more orthodox. Instead of starting at the beginning of a hunt and going on to the end, with sundry interferences, he was approaching the mystery from both ends, anticipating the solution somewhere in the middle.

The Chamberlain angle was equally unusual.

Despite the fact that McNab had Chamberlain under some kind of supervision, the fur importer was outwardly possessed of an unblemished reputation. Yet the Toff *knew* that as a consort of men like Dougall and Hi Ling he was a dangerous criminal. The only previous communication he had had with the man was the affair of the visiting-card. Chamberlain's attitude suggested that he was not going to pretend that he did not know what Rollison was after, but was going to bluff.

He sat and stared at the Toff, his hands clenched in characteristic position, although he did not realise that it gave him away. The Toff was smiling, and smoke was curling from his lips. In silver greys, he was immaculate; and the sun striking through an open window shone on his sleek, black hair.

'What *are* you drivelling about?' demanded Chamberlain at last.

'Not bad,' said Rollison cheerfully. 'In fact you might put it across with some people, Chamberlain. Country houses or no country houses, you're heading for a nasty fall in the very near future.'

'Don't talk nonsense. If anyone's going to fall it's you.'

'Oh, I have. Underneath a car,' retorted the Toff. 'Strange how things won't work according to plan, isn't it? Actually I've never been impressed by Nigger and Hi Ling. Certainly not in the first flight, and they're somewhat too easily scared. Like other people I know.'

Chamberlain drew a deep breath.

'I don't know what you're talking about, Rollison. If there's anything you've got to say with any sense in it, I'll listen. If there isn't, I'm too busy to waste time. I had some silly card with your name on—I suppose you are the same man?'

'Yes, I'm the same man,' said Rollison, and chuckled. 'Chamberlain, you may be a bad crook, but you're a fair actor. A pity I'm not in much doubt about you, isn't it?'

Chamberlain straightened his glasses.

'I think it's time you went.'

'Oh, not yet,' said the Toff. 'I've several other things to say. A word of warning to start with—you should be more careful when you go to the "Steam Packet".'

Chamberlain's hands clenched.

'What on earth—'

'Suppose you stop fooling?' asked Rollison, and his voice hardened. 'If you're running away with the idea that I don't know what you do and what you're doing, you can lose it. All I'm looking for is enough evidence to make a police charge advisable, and that's not going to be long in coming.' His eyes were hard as he spoke, and he could see the effort Chamberlain was making to keep his self-control. He knew that he was frightening the fur importer. Psychological terrorism would always be the Toff's best weapon.

'I—I've never broken a law in my life!' snapped Chamberlain.

'Then you don't know much about the law,' said the Toff gently. 'Get a nodding acquaintance with it, it might save your neck. Not that I think that's likely. Chamberlain, it was a foolish thing to mutilate the hands. There's just one reason why hands should be mutilated and that's to prevent identification. You told the world as well as me and the police that the man you killed was known on police records, and—'

Chamberlain cracked.

He pushed his chair back, sending it crashing to the floor, and rounded his desk quickly, his hands clenched.

'Get out of here, get out! Come to my office talking a lot of nonsense like this—I'll smash your ruddy face in! I'll—'

He struck out wildly.

The Toff, who seemed to be in his chair one moment and on his feet the next, side-stepped with ease, and delivered a short-arm jab to the side of Chamberlain's ribs. Enough to sting but not to damage. Chamberlain stopped himself and swung round to deliver another punch. It hummed past the Toff's head, and the Toff rapped a sharp blow to the solar plexus. Chamberlain gasped and doubled up.

The Toff stepped back a pace and watched silently, waited until he was sure that Chamberlain could hear, and said gently: 'Very foolish, Chamberlain, from start to finish. That's a little indication of how badly hurt you're going to be, particularly if Sylvia Sanderson meets trouble.'

He spoke slowly, so that each word impinged itself on Chamberlain's ears. And then he backed towards the door, moving silently and with a speed that seemed unnatural. One moment Chamberlain saw him, lean-faced and with his eyes agleam with mockery. The next he was gone, the door closed.

On the face of Arnold Chamberlain there were varying emotions. Of pain and hatred – and fear.

Primarily fear.

Rollison walked slowly down the stairs of the building, through the showrooms, where there was evidence of a considerable and thriving business. But not a business enough to make Chamberlain really wealthy.

As he reached the thronged pavements of Oxford Street Rollison saw two things: the man with the squint, whom he did not yet know as Jaggers, and the two plain-clothes men, who made a great point of neither seeing nor recognising the Toff.

Rollison smiled as he walked towards Gresham Terrace.

It was less what he had seen in Oxford Street than what he was seeing in his mind that concerned him then, however. For it had come with a quite surprising suddenness – a factor that might be the common denominator of this mystery.

Sanderson ran a small Australasian shipping line.

Hi Ling and Dougall ran a similar one in England.

Chamberlain would have to ship most of his furs from abroad, and might easily run one or two ships. There were dozens – in fact hundreds – of small firms operating a virtual 'pirate' service of cargo boats, with the idea of cutting their own transport costs and making a side-profit from the carrying of other goods.

How to find out?

Rollison was reluctant at the time to consult further with McNab. The Scotsman had, so far, been very obliging, but he might easily contrive to do something which would complicate matters for the Toff. By putting the plain-clothes men to watch Chamberlain he had done precisely what the Toff wanted – added a reason for Chamberlain to lose his nerve. He wanted Chamberlain to do that, very badly.

But for the rest he preferred to carry on alone.

He turned into Gresham Terrace at about half-past five, and as he entered his flat he heard the telephone ringing. He lifted it, wondering as he did so where Brendon was, and hoping that the youngster had not gone far.

Jolly's voice came.

'About Lowerby, sir. He has gone in the London direction. I have been trying to call you for nearly an hour.'

'Right,' said Rollison. 'Nothing more?'

'Nothing, sir. I understand' – Jolly paused, with a nicety of judgment – 'that Sir George Manering's XI is in a bad way, sir—nearly two hundred behind with only five wickets to fall.'

Rollison chuckled.

'A sad week, my Jolly. All right, come back to town.'

'Are you sure it won't be advisable for me to wait for the return of the doctor, sir?'

'No, I'm not. But I've got a job for you here, Jolly, and even you can't be in two places at once.'

'I will start immediately, sir.'

'Do,' said the Toff.

He closed down, made sure that Brendon was not in one of the other rooms, and then went out again. He took a taxi this time, but went again to the showrooms of Arnold Chamberlain. He was prepared to wait, if necessary, for an hour. He needed less than half.

Dr. Vincent Lowerby drove up, parked his Morris in a side-turning, and then stopped for some minutes while getting something from the back seats. Rollison watched without appearing to, and saw the doctor take out a small table, with the legs and surface covered in brown paper. Lowerby carried it quickly towards Chamberlain's shop and disappeared.

Rollison rubbed his chin.

'Jolly,' he said aloud, 'you found more than you know. A visit to Hersham and Mr. Meer is indicated. Meer—odd name. I wonder if Mannering knows him?' Rollison chuckled. 'George won't be in the best of moods if they've lost today.'

The affair of the faked Sheraton table – faked, if Jolly was right, and it was not a matter on which Jolly was likely to fall down – was of considerable interest, although so far its importance could not be estimated. But here was a direct connection between Meer – so far unknown in the affair – Lowerby, and Chamberlain.

Chamberlain was not a man to buy fakes.

There was, therefore, something more than intrinsic value – or worthlessness – in the deal in antiques.

Was it the first of such deals?

That being a point on which there was no available evidence, the Toff wasted little time on it as he returned to the flat. He thought more of young Brendon, who had, after all, left the flat and could hardly be blamed for it. With a youth of Brendon's type, and one so obviously anxious to be up and doing, the present inactivity would be unbearable.

Had he gone to try something on his own?

Rollison sighed.

He stopped thinking as he reached the landing outside his flat. For it was occupied not by Brendon but by the tall and chunky figure of Chief Inspector McNab, whose sandy eyebrows were drawn together as he scowled.

'Why, Mac, pleasures do come sometimes.'

'Pleasures?' grunted McNab. 'Dinna waste ye're words on me, Rollison. I know well what ye're thinking. I'd like a word or two with you.'

'Have I ever been known to refuse you yet?' asked the Toff.

McNab, who did not appear to be in a good humour, grunted a non-committal reply. A whisky-and-soda, a comfortable chair and a cigarette did little to thaw him, and he lost no time in getting down to business.

'About this Hersham murder, Rolleeson. Have ye learned anything worth the knowing?'

'I wouldn't say so; no. Have you?'

'It's time there were some results,' McNab said, and the Toff knew in that moment that Higher Powers had been urging the Scotsman to greater endeavours. Without admitting that in so many words, McNab pointed out glumly that there had been no developments whatsoever. He even admitted that he had questioned Dougall and Hi Ling, but that they had presented excellent alibis.

'They'd be good at that,' said the Toff. 'What have you come for, Mac, apart from just to swop stories?'

McNab glowered.

'I'm not swopping stories, Rolleeson. Ye've been active, I know that, and I'd like to know why.'

'Finding dead ends while looking for clues,' smiled the Toff. 'I can't give you anything in the way of evidence. All I can offer is a hunch, and I'm not going to do that—you don't like hunches, and no decent policeman admits they exist. I—'

The telephone rang sharply.

Rollison excused himself and lifted the receiver. He heard Brendon's voice at the other end of the wire, and judging from it Brendon was excited. If the Toff's expression remained inscrutable for McNab's benefit, he felt his heart jump.

'It's true, I tell you!' snapped Brendon. 'I saw him not ten minutes ago, and I'm outside the place he went into now. Jim Sanderson's in London!'

Chapter Fourteen

Fast Work

If it were true – and the Toff could not say that it was not – it was the first real break that had come his way since the start of the affair, even if it smashed one theory. He said easily: 'All right, old man—what's the address?'

'I'm at the corner of Queen's Road and Bayswater Road, near the station,' said Brendon. 'I checked up on that before ringing through, Jim went into a house not two minutes' walk away.'

'Did you inquire there?' Rollison was getting the essential questions over in a cool voice that might have been discussing any subject, and McNab certainly had no reason for imagining that it was connected with the case of the murdered tramp. Brendon felt irritated at the calmness with which his news was received, but said evenly enough: 'No; I thought you ought to know.'

'That's fine,' said Rollison; 'and you're quite right. I'll certainly be calling before long.'

He replaced the receiver, eyed McNab while obviously not looking at him, and then apologised.

'Sorry, Mac. Other things will intrude. I wish I could help you, but I can't yet.'

McNab looked his doubts, but made no comment. The Toff saw him out, and then looked from the window overlooking the street. McNab had not gone away immediately, but was hesitating outside. Probably he was wondering whether Rollison was going out on an errand connected with the mystery.

'My Mac,' murmured the Toff, 'you're getting at once cunning and obvious. However …'

He stepped through the kitchen quarters of the flat sad down the fire-escape ladder leading to a courtyard which served the whole block. In five minutes he was walking briskly along Piccadilly, while McNab was still hesitating in Gresham Terrace.

A cab took the Toff to Bayswater Road Station in less than fifteen minutes, despite a traffic block. Frank Brendon was standing outside a near-by fruiters', his hands thrust deep into his pockets, and his expression pugnacious.

'Well, you didn't lose much time,' he admitted. 'You sounded as though it didn't matter a damn.'

'I had visitors,' said the Toff briefly. 'Are you sure of this?'

'I saw him with my own eyes,' said Brendon, 'and I wouldn't make a mistake like that. Damn it, Sylvia might be around. I—I had a hell of a job not to bust in, Rollison.'

'I'm glad you didn't; but what stopped you?'

'Well …' Brendon hesitated. 'When all's said and done, if you're right about Jim, and he's worried by something, I don't want to do anything silly.'

A reasonable explanation, thought Rollison, and it showed that Brendon could use his head. It proved, also, that he was worried by the possibility that Jim Sanderson was frightened of the law – or of something less understandable.

For the moment the fact that he had seen Sanderson go into the house along Queen's Road was the thing that mattered.

'Number 29a,' said Brendon. 'He got out of a cab, and I saw him as he paid the man off. I was right up here, but I can swear to it being Sanderson.'

'Good. What brought you here?'

Brendon shrugged.

'It was an amazing stroke of luck. I'd read an advertisement about some photographic stuff on sale at Whiteley's, and I wanted to have a look at it. I'm mad-keen on the camera, you know.'

Rollison eyed him keenly.

'That all?'

'Of course it's all. What else should there be?'

'I don't know,' admitted the Toff, and did not add that he was always suspicious when the gods seemed to drop manna on to his lap. But at least it was possible, and coincidences often happened; a fact he sometimes pointed out to McNab.

Nevertheless he was aware of an uncomfortable feeling that Brendon might not be telling the whole truth. Nor did he dismiss the possibility, although he did nothing more to suggest that he had doubts of the other's story.

'What are you going to do?' asked Brendon.

'Call and ask for Sanderson,' said the Toff promptly. 'It will serve some purpose, anyhow. You stay within sight, but on the other side of the road, will you?'

Brendon agreed.

The Toff went to the door of Number 29a and rang the bell. There was a pause before footsteps shuffled towards the door, and after a lapse of thirty seconds it opened. An old man, wearing a ragged smoking-jacket with lapels liberally stained, wizened-face, and affecting a straggly, nicotine-embellished moustache, eyed him with rheumy, unwelcoming eyes.

'Yes?'

'Good evening,' said the Toff amiably. 'I believe a Mr. Sanderson is staying here. May I—'

'You believe wrong,' said the ancient. 'Never heard of anyone o' that name here, an' I've lived around for forty years come Michaelmas.'

'Really?' said the Toff, and he seemed surprised. 'But I was assured that Mr. Sanderson—'

'You were assured wrong, young man. I haven't any time to waste, so—'

'It's hardly wasting time,' the Toff said easily. 'I am a police officer, and a man answering the description of a James Sanderson is believed to be staying here.' He still spoke affably, even though he knew that if his statement was challenged it might lead to some difficulties. It was not the first time he had represented himself to be a C.I.D. man, and he did not expect that it would be the last.

The ancient looked startled for the first time.

'The police, are you? Well, why didn't you say so? Where's your card?'

The Toff put his hand to his pocket and half withdrew his wallet. As he expected, the ancient waved it away, and rubbed a wrinkled hand across his moustache.

'Never mind. I know a policeman when I sees one; I thought you was from the start. You want to see the register, I suppose? Not that I've got to keep one by law; this isn't a hotel, it's a boarding-house for private people, that's all. But come *in,* don't stand there all the time. I don't want all Queen's Road to know my business.'

He stood aside, and the Toff entered a narrow, gloomy passage-cum-hallway. In a drawer of a table standing in a recess was the register, and the ancient took it out and opened it for the Toff to read. Rollison glanced at the four signatures that had been entered during the last ten days. Certainly the name of Sanderson was not among them, but—

He glanced up at the ancient.

And he had one of the major shocks of his life, for he also glanced up at an automatic held unwaveringly in the ancient's hand.

At no time would the Toff admit that he should have been prepared for that.

There were occasions when he had made mistakes, and he was always the first to admit them. But to find the automatic there, to know that he was threatened by the ancient, came with a shock of real surprise.

'Police!' snapped the ancient. 'I could see *you* wasn't a mile off! Don't move your hands! I—Come on, Charlie, hurry up! There's a gentleman wants some attention.'

Charlie – obviously summoned by bell, for the old man had not raised his voice – loomed out of the gloom of the passage near the foot of the stairs. The Toff made him out to be a burly, broad-shouldered man whose face was in the shadows; he was one of the roughnecks of the 'Steam Packet'.

The shock was over.

The Toff's mind was beginning to work on more normal lines, and he realised the implications of this affair. Sanderson, if it had been Sanderson, was in this house which was occupied by Hi Ling's hirelings. It showed the wideness of Hi Ling's scope, it suggested that Brendon had been right.

And if he had, then Sanderson was in some way connected with the Hi Ling enterprise.

No more than a minute had passed since he had first seen the gun. Now he smiled, and spoke amiably, as if nothing untoward had happened.

'Nice goings-on, little man. You did that well.'

'I do everything well,' said the old one gruffly. 'And I don't want none o' your lip. I—What's the matter, Charlie?'

For Charlie had uttered a single, expressive oath.

The Toff knew why, knew that he had been recognised. It had its amusing side to see the startled expression on the roughneck's face, but he had little cause for amusement. The old one was between him and the door, Charlie between him and the stairs. In the narrow passage there was no room for free action, and he felt then that he was trapped – for the time being at least.

It was not a nice feeling.

'What—' began the ancient again.

'It's the *Torf!*' gasped Charlie. 'I—'

And then Rollison moved.

He knew that if he did not get away now there was small chance of his ever doing so. He kicked backwards towards the ancient, hitting the man on the shin sharply enough to make him gasp and to lower his gun. At the same moment he lunged forward and struck at the roughneck. His fist connected, but not heavily. A wild kick caught him on the knee and sent an excruciating pain through his leg. He tried to ignore it, swung round and tried to pass the ancient, but his knee gave way and he almost fell.

Staggering, he saw the old one raise the gun, butt foremost.

Nothing Rollison could do could stop it, and the butt crashed on to the back of his neck. There was only a split second between realization of what was coming and the actuality. He felt the blow, the resultant pain – and then he thumped down.

The ancient kicked him, once vigorously and once as if he enjoyed doing it.

'Get him upstairs,' he said. 'Go on, Charlie. The Toff, is it? Won't Hi Ling be pleased?'

Hi Ling was pleased.

He received the message by telephone while at the office of the Dougall-Ling Shipping Company, and at first he found it hard to believe. Convinced, he gave orders that the Toff should be kept at 29a Queen's Road until he was able to get there, and he did not have to emphasise the need for tying Rollison securely and making sure that he could not escape.

'Did you see anyone else?' he asked the ancient.

'There's a young fella hanging around, but I'm not sure he was with Rollison.'

'Young fellow—he is fair, and square-shouldered, and he looks angry?'

'Well, that's a good guess.' The ancient seemed startled.

'My fliend,' said Hi Ling softly, 'take word yourself to that young man and tell him Mr. Rollison wishes to see him at the house immediately. Get him inside, and do precisely the same as you did to Rollison. I shall want them both, you understand?'

'All right, I'll do that.'

The ancient shuffled down the steps of the house, seeing Brendon on the opposite side of the road, staring at him with patent curiosity. He beckoned, and Brendon walked over, with no idea of what might happen. To him it seemed obvious that Rollison had sent a message of sorts.

'Excuse me, sir,' said the ancient respectfully, 'but the gentleman who just called said that he would like you to come in at once. He says the matter is most urgent.'

'Right-ho!' said Brendon, and he did not know whether to be pleased or relieved. At least it suggested that Rollison had found something.

Was Sanderson inside?

If so, would he explain why he and Sylvia had disappeared?

Brendon stepped over the threshold, and did not see the leg of the roughneck stretched out to trip him up. He went sprawling, the door closed abruptly, and the butt of a revolver descended effectively on the nape of his neck.

Chapter Fifteen

Unfortunate For Chamberlain

Mr. Arnold Chamberlain had been lucky in many respects in his association with Hi Ling and Dougall.

Those two gentlemen of the criminal profession, although they had not been active in England long, had for many years had associations in London, and had turned them to advantage quickly. The boarding-house in Bayswater was an excellent hiding-place for aliens who were smuggled into the country, and who wished not to report daily – or weekly or monthly – to the police. It was also a clearing-house for other smuggled goods, and the ancient was an efficient manager, receiving good pay, and yet satisfied to leave the reins of control in someone else's hands.

Chamberlain, on starting his connection with the other two, had realised the possible value of the house in Bays-water, and he had used it on occasions. But the last thing he had expected was that Rollison should walk into the house and virtually offer himself for slaughter.

Like Hi Ling, he found it hard to believe.

When he was finally convinced, he took off his horn-rimmed glasses and passed a hand across his forehead. Then he grinned. Then he began to laugh – low pitched, effective laughter which hit loudly against Hi Ling's ears and did not please the Chinaman. He quietened at last, and: 'Very nice work, Hi Ling, that's very good indeed. Now we've got nothing to worry about, nothing. What are you doing with them—both of them? By hell, it's good to believe!'

'I am keeping them for you,' said Hi Ling. 'There is much Rollison may know. He may have told others. It will be well to ask questions.'

'He won't be a talker.'

Hi Ling said softly: 'I can find ways of making even the great Rollison talk, my fliend, have no fears of that. A little pain—perhaps a little more. But it is important you should come soon. We do not require the two men alive too long. There is always a chance that waiting men will prove a mistake.'

'I'll be over. Where will you have them?'

'It is quite safe at Queen's Road. There is a cellar, and no sounds will get through.'

'Eight o'clock,' said Chamberlain. 'Prompt!'

He replaced the receiver, sat back and chuckled to himself, lit a cigarette, and then considered the Sheraton table which Lowerby had brought. Lowerby had not been in the office many minutes before Chamberlain had agreed to buy the table for eighty pounds, showing the doctor a handsome profit. Lowerby could not understand how Chamberlain was so easily taken in, for even he knew that it was not genuine.

It did not occur to Lowerby that Mr. Meer should have known also. Lowerby was one of those men who were always so satisfied with their own self-efficiency that it did not occur to them to think beyond it. As far as he knew, he was co-operating with Chamberlain chiefly on the matter of illegal supplies of drugs, and other things which loomed less important. The buying and selling of the antiques was a side-line that made him feel that he was putting one over Chamberlain, and delighted him.

Chamberlain also seemed delighted as he examined the table.

He ran his thumb along the bottom ledge of the surrounds, and suddenly touched a slight protuberance. He pressed harder, heard a faint whirring sound, and saw a small drawer that opened abruptly. In the drawer was a wash-leather bag. In the bag were several small diamonds and a ruby of quite unusual size.

Chamberlain examined them, and chuckled with satisfaction.

And then, with the drawer open, and the jewels on the surface of the table, the door opened.

Chamberlain heard the preliminary tap on it, and made a grab at the gems, but he was too late. On the threshold stood the two C.I.D. men who had been watching the showrooms.

Chamberlain did not know that McNab, urged by the Assistant Commissioner to quicker results, had ordered his men to interrogate Chamberlain on a comparatively minor matter – the payment of duty on some of his furs. He had also given instructions for the visit to be made without warning – but even McNab, in his wildest moments of optimism, did not dream of the evidence of crime available.

The C.I.D. men saw the table, the open drawer and the jewels.

There was nothing in the world to prevent Chamberlain claiming that they were his, that he had every right to hide them as he wanted to. In different circumstances, and had the Toff not already alarmed him, he might have tried the bluff, although it would have been a bad moment. As it was, he stared at the two young, determined-looking plain-clothes men, and there was ample evidence of alarm and guilt in his expression. It had happened at the one moment when Chamberlain's defences were down – and that was partly due to his good humour at the knowledge of the Toff's coming fate.

The taller man spoke brusquely.

'I'd like you to explain those, sir.'

Chamberlain snapped: 'What the hell are you doing here? I— '

'We are police officers.' said the spokesman, and he did not propose to allow what seemed a glorious chance of a triumph to pass out of his hands. He was prepared even to bluff, without, of course, doing anything against police regulations. And there was nothing against asking questions, or opening a door after tapping on it.

'Why, you—' snarled Chamberlain.

It was a moment when he was liable to lose his head, when the training of years was likely to come uppermost. Not for the first time Chamberlain was faced with police and a situation that opened the gates of a gaol. Not for the first time did he act as he did then.

He snatched a Luger from a shoulder-holster.

Both men looked startled; they had no time to be afraid.

'Now then, don't—'

Chamberlain fired the silenced automatic.

He touched the trigger four times, and each bullet found a home. Both men fell, their faces showing the utter surprise that reached them just before death. Small round holes showed in their foreheads; both reared up oddly before they crumpled up. Their falling made two distinct thudding sounds on the thick carpet; the blood oozing from their heads began to spread.

Chamberlain stared down for a moment, expressionless.

Then he stepped towards them. He touched their wrists, made sure that their pulses were not beating, and drew back. From a cloak-room he fetched a towel and slipped it beneath their heads to prevent the blood staining the carpet. Then he sat back at his desk and began to think.

And he knew he had made a fateful mistake; he might have got away with the killing in the States, but there he would have had a network of gangster-lawyers as well as graft-rotten police to help him. Even they were lessening in the States – the chief reason he had come abroad.

Now …

He knew that in the moment of alarm he had reverted to type. The ingrained instinct of the killer had revealed itself, as it had done in the earlier days of Prohibition *in* Chicago. He had killed mercilessly and without warning, but he had to face the consequences of that in the best-policed country in the world.

Cold sweat beaded Chamberlain's forehead.

He seemed to feel the handcuffs about his wrists.

He saw that it was impossible to stay here. The place was lost to him and all there was in it. The Yard would be inquiring very quickly about the two missing detectives. He might have less than an hour in which to work.

He pressed a bell, and his finger was unsteady. As he waited he filled a glass with whisky and drank off half of it at a stretch. The door opened and Jaggers stepped in, to stop in sudden alarm at the sight of the bodies.

'Gawd! Boss—'

'Don't waste time!' snapped Chamberlain. 'They'd come to pick me up. Have someone over from the "Steam Packet" in a hurry, and get the bodies into a big packing-case. Have a van round to take it to Aldgate; Hi Ling will look after it.'

'Oo-kay,' muttered Jaggers; but his eyes would not leave the two dead men.

'Move in a hustle!' snapped Chamberlain. 'We've got to be out of here in half an hour.'

Jaggers disappeared.

Chamberlain took his keys from his pocket and opened the wall-safe behind his desk. He wasted no time in looking through the papers and other things, but crammed them into a suit-case he had waiting and empty. He took every paper that could possibly betray him from the desk, then went into the three rooms that served him as a flat and did the same. It took him twenty-five minutes, and when he went back into the office Jaggers and a man from Aldgate were lifting the bodies and putting them into a big packing-case, normally containing furs for import or export.

'All right,' Chamberlain said, as the bodies were inside. 'Nail it down safely and then get away. Keep it at the "Steam Packet" for the time being, or at the docks. Don't do anything until you've heard from Hi Ling.'

'Okay,' said Jaggers. Used to violence as he was, this had scared him. Killings did not matter; the chance of being found out did, and Jaggers had a healthy regard for the effectiveness of the London C.I.D. 'Where do I find you, Boss?'

'I'll get in touch when I want you. Here's something to be going on with.' Chamberlain had left a wad of one-pound notes on the desk, and he handed them to the man with the squint. 'That's a hundred. Keep right away from this place, understand?'

'Ye-ep. But, Boss, Rollison—'

For the first time since the entry of the police Chamberlain laughed, and it was not pleasant to hear.

'He's all right. Don't worry about that.'

'But—'

'Hi Ling's got him,' he snapped. 'Don't argue.'

Jaggers stared.

'He's got—Gawd, I don't believe it!'

Chamberlain swore at him, and went out of the office. He did not go into Oxford Street, but through a rear entrance into a side-street, where he walked swiftly to Piccadilly Circus. Judging it safe to hire a cab from there, he was driven to Bayswater Road Station, where he alighted, paid the cab, and then walked towards Number 29a.

He was not followed.

Now that it had happened he felt calm enough, and capable of dealing with any emergency. But he had to work fast; the need was greater even than before.

But he did not propose to let the unexpected development put him off the Sanderson job. Nor the Toff …

Rollison had started this.

Until he had interfered there had been not the slightest suggestion of trouble from the police. The first signs of it had followed on the Toff's heels, but that would have been a lot more worrying if Rollison had been free.

Chamberlain laughed aloud as he entered the house, and was greeted first by the ancient and then Hi Ling, who was in an upstairs room.

'Rollison,' said Hi Ling, 'is next door, mistah. And Brendon is, too.'

'Let's get them handled,' said Chamberlain sharply. 'Have them taken downstairs, and don't waste any time about it. Do everything short of tearing his tongue out; he wants that for speaking with.'

Hi Ling laughed.

'He shall talk, mistah; do not worry about that.'

Chief Inspector Horace McNab was not a man who did things on the spur of the moment. He had decided that if there were no results from his talk with Rollison he would start working more openly against Chamberlain, who, the past few days had helped to prove, was not unconnected with certain undesirable elements in the East End.

McNab expected a report by seven o'clock. It did not come.

By eight his men were still missing.

At half past he went with a sergeant to the Oxford Street showrooms, but found no one – not even a caretaker – in. The flat which Chamberlain used as living-quarters appeared to be empty, and without a warrant McNab hesitated to break in. At considerable risk to his self-esteem, he telephoned the Assistant Commissioner and reported. That gentleman suggested McNab came to see him. McNab obliged, taking with him the evidence of a patrol policeman that the two C.I.D. officers had been seen entering the showrooms, but had not been seen to come out.

A warrant was signed.

The premises were broken open and searched, but there was no one in them, no signs of the two C.I.D. men's presence. There were signs of hurried departure, however, while McNab, always a thorough officer, fancied he saw a damp patch in the middle of a thick-piled modern Indian carpet. At his suggestion the stain was examined by a police surgeon, the moisture was extracted and taken for analysis. Within two hours the assurance that it was human blood was given by the pathologist who had been urged to work so late, and for the first time McNab allowed himself to consider the possibility of more murder.

He went to see Rollison.

All he found was Jolly, who of course revealed very little, but did go as far as to say that he had expected to find his employer in.

McNab was more than usually brusque.

'All right, Jolly. Have him call me at my house the moment he gets in touch with you. Make sure of it.'

'Very good, sir.' Jolly closed the door behind the inspector but did not grimace at his thoughts of McNab, whom he secretly considered to have the intelligence of an ox – which was unjust.

For Jolly was worried about Rollison.

Chapter Sixteen

Methods Of Persuasion

The Toff had many rules – and often said that he obeyed none of them. That was not strictly true, for he followed his own principles faithfully, although he knew many variations of them. One essential, however, was that of facing facts; nothing was gained by pretending things were not as they were; he had always maintained that, and had a habit of advising others on the same point.

He faced facts that evening.

He recovered consciousness half an hour after he had been knocked out, and for the first ten minutes he had been concerned only with the aching in his head and the painful burning at his eyes. They had eased eventually, and he had found that his hands and feet were bound, that he was lying on a bed, that the room was in darkness, and he was not alone.

The soft breathing of another prisoner came clearly to his ears.

He waited five minutes before he tried to call out – although a handkerchief tied tightly across his lips made clear utterance impossible. He contrived a sound that earned no response three times in quick succession.

Whoever was with him was asleep or unconscious. The Toff reasoned that the latter was more likely, and also that it might be Brendon. He thought again of the youngster's story.

Had he been at Queen's Road by sheer chance?

Or had he lied?

Rollison believed that it was most likely that he had told a half-truth, and fancied that Brendon had had some reason for going to Whiteley's or nearby. It was even possible that he had deliberately lured the Toff to Number 29a. That might explain the fact that he had waited for the Toff instead of doing what was more typical of him and going like a bull at a gate to the house.

The Toff disliked the theory, but had to admit its possibility.

He could see daylight through a faint gap in the curtains that covered the window, but that meant little, for the June days were long, and daylight would last until nearly ten o'clock. He had entered the house, as nearly as he could judge, at seven o'clock. All the daylight did was to tell him he had not been unconscious more than two and a half hours.

And then, after a silence that had seemed to be unending, after a sequence of futile thoughts, he heard a sound. The sound grew more distinct, and he knew that footsteps were echoing on a flight of stairs. In a few seconds he heard them more clearly, and knew they were approaching the room.

A key was inserted in the lock.

The door opened and light filled the small room in which he was imprisoned. It was typical of him that he did not look immediately towards the door but to the small bed alongside that on which he was lying. He saw Brendon, in the same fix as himself, but still unconscious, and he knew that the youngster had not played any part in a trick to get him here. The fact relieved his mind of one anxiety.

He looked at the newcomers narrowly.

There were two – the roughneck he had already met and Nigger Dougall. Dougall was smiling, and it was not a nice smile. He looked at the Toff, and his lips turned further back, but he did not speak. Instead he showed a knife that he was carrying, while the roughneck cut the cords at Rollison's feet and pushed his legs to the floor.

'Get up an' walk,' said Dougall.

The Toff found his legs unsteady, and his ankles painful, hut he contrived to move towards the door.

'That's enough,' snapped Dougall. 'Don't make no mistakes, Roll'son, you ain't got a chance in hel've getting away.'

With his hands tied behind him and the gag across his mouth the Toff was prepared to admit the point. He stood unsteadily while Brendon was roughly awakened by the simple expedient of pouring a jug of water over his face. Brendon was dragged to his feet, and the two prisoners were forced to go downstairs. There were three flights, all difficult to negotiate, but Brendon stumbled more than the Toff, who was trying not to think.

A narrow passage, and then more stairs, obviously leading to a cellar. Rollison went steadily onwards, and as they reached the bottom of the steps heard Chamberlain's voice. The words were spoken softly, but he caught the drift: 'Well, it's done, and you've got to get rid've the bodies. Understand that?'

Hi Ling said softly: 'Most foolish, Chamberlain. Policemen are bad men to kill.'

'Never mind that, I—Keep quiet!'

Chamberlain had heard the sound of approach, and when the Toff was pushed into the cellar, which was brilliantly lighted but poorly furnished as well as dusty, the American was looking towards the door. He was sitting on a wooden chair, and Hi Ling was standing imperturbably by him.

Chamberlain's eyes glittered as Dougall removed Rollison's gag.

'Awake, are you, Rollison?'

'And alive, for some odd reason,' said the Toff. It was the truth that he did not expect to get out of the house alive, although he was prepared to snatch at the slightest chance if it were offered. He knew that the only reason he had not been killed off-hand was that he had frightened Chamberlain by hinting at knowledge which others might have learned.

Chamberlain laughed.

'Don't you worry about that. We don't kill for the sake of it. I want to have a talk with you.'

'It's nice to be friendly,' said the Toff.

'Not too much mouth.' Chamberlain glanced at Hi Ling, who had pushed Brendon into a chair, for the youngster was finding it difficult to keep on his feet. Rollison was steady, and he glanced at the Chinaman, who was smoking a newly lit cigarette. 'You don't have to worry—'

'Why not save yourself time and trouble?' asked the Toff amiably, and he showed no sign of the fear that was in him – a fear of both pain and death, which he had never claimed he did not possess. It was man's reaction under fear, not fear itself, that branded some folk cowards. 'I'm not talking. What I know and others know just isn't coming to you.'

'Don't be a fool, Rollison. There's no need to get annoyed because—'

The Toff chuckled – and to those watching, even Hi Ling, it was something to demand admiration, particularly after he had spoken again.

'Chamberlain, give me credit for a little common sense. This is a cellar, and sounds won't travel. Hi Ling comes of a country which specialises in methods of persuasion. I've never seen him smoking before, and I know what he's got the cigarette for. Most painful, especially beneath the arms.

'You're cool!' exclaimed Chamberlain.

'It is a brave man, yes,' said Hi Ling. 'One could salute you, Rollison. But …' He shrugged. 'Remove his coat, Dougall, and other clothes.'

Rollison kept his balance while his wrist-bonds were cut, his coat, waistcoat, shirt and singlet were stripped off him, Brendon – also ungagged – was staring up, his eyes filled with horror, as if he could not believe what was going to happen. The calmness in the cellar, the utter lack of fear by Rollison, or feeling in the others, were enough to hypnotise most men, and they did Brendon.

'I will talk,' said Hi Ling. 'Rollison, you have some knowledge. You will answer questions. Why did you go to this house?'

'Now that,' said the Toff, 'is asking. I was interested in all your movements, Hi Ling. A respectable house—'

'Lying will not help. You asked for a man.'

The Toff looked surprised.

'Did I? Oh, yes; but I needed an excuse, I—'

Hi Ling moved his hand. Dougall, close to the Toff, gripped his wrist and twisted his arm behind his back, causing a sharp, excruciating pain which made the Toff gasp. Brendon exclaimed, but no one else made a sound, while Chamberlain's eyes were fixed on the Toff's.

'Why did you think any one man was here?' asked Hi Ling.

The Toff said nothing.

He was facing the inevitable, and knew it. Either now or in ten minutes they would ask a question that he would not answer, and he had given up all hope of bluffing Hi Ling. To answer anything at all was useless, it merely prolonged the ordeal, would make these men believe that under sufficient pressure he would crack.

The twisting of his arm increased.

He tightened his lips against the pain, and his forehead was suddenly beaded with sweat, but he gave no answer. Hi Ling stepped forward and moved the lighted cigarette towards the pit of Rollison's arm, until the heat could be felt by the bared flesh.

'Why, Rollison?'

Rollison forced a smile.

Hi Line took the cigarette a fraction nearer.

'Why?

'Oh, God!' gasped Brendon. I can't stand this! I'd seen Sanderson come in here. I told him, I—'

Hi Ling stepped back a pace, and there was triumph in his eyes. Chamberlain had leaned forward, his clenched fists on the rickety table in front of him in that characteristic, tell-tale attitude. He said slowly: 'What do you know of Sanderson, Rollison?'

The Toff shrugged his free shoulder, an odd gesture.

'You're not getting any satisfaction from me,' he said levelly. 'You'd be wise to believe it, for otherwise it's a waste of time. Brendon doesn't know anything of the slightest importance; making him crack won't help you. You've met something you can't get past. Chamberlain, and if you kill us …' He shrugged again, and there was a hard light in his eyes. It takes you a step nearer to the gallows, that's all.'

'You damned fool—'

'Talk is so easy,' said Hi Ling gently. 'A little persuasion will make you think so diff'lently, Rollison.'

He pushed the cigarette home.

Rollison started, and the pain sheered through him. There was a faint smell of burning hair and flesh. The cigarette stayed there, the pain grew almost unbearable, but he tightened his lips and gritted his teeth. He heard Brendon crying wildly that they must stop, even saw the roughneck kick at Brendon as the Australian tried to get up.

He felt weak with pain, but his eyes met Hi Ling's evenly, until at last the Chinaman stepped back.

'So. We shall need to go further, Rollison. You are most foolish.'

'Why the hell don't you talk?' snapped Chamberlain. 'I've got nothing against you. I'm clearing out of the country and at the end of a week you can go free.'

'Free?' mocked the Toff. 'I know Hi Ling and Dougall too well, Chamberlain; soft soap won't work. The quicker you realise I'm not talking the quicker this business will be over. Got that?'

Chamberlain stared in silence.

Hi Ling shrugged, and slipped a small knife from his pocket – he was still dressed in European clothes.

'Push his hand to the front, Dougall.'

Dougall obeyed. The movement of his arm caused a sharp pain at the burned spot, but Rollison said nothing as Dougall held his hand outwards. The fingers were steady; there was no shaking.

'Beneath the finger-nails,' Hi Ling said, 'it is most—'

He did not finish, but the knife moved forward. Chamberlain seemed hardly to be breathing, Brendon was swearing, Dougall was grinning, and the roughneck turned his face away.

Chapter Seventeen

Nightmare

To the Toff it was a nightmare.

The temptation to talk was overwhelming, but he knew that he had to fight it back. The one hope of forcing these men into a fatal error was to keep them afraid.

If they knew what he knew they would no longer be that.

They would kill him. No matter what they promised in the effort to make him talk, as soon as this was over he would be murdered, and Brendon with him. There was no chance at all of any other result, and it would be better to die with the knowledge that psychological terrorism could still be effective than with the knowledge that they would go on without the fear of what he had told the police or others.

Had there seemed the slightest chance of saving his or Brendon's life he would have talked.

There was none.

If help came it would be from the outside, and there was not the slightest probability of it.

He felt the silence in the cellar, the tenseness of the atmosphere. He watched the knife approaching his fingers with an almost impersonal, indifferent gaze.

And then the interruption came.

It was no more than a light tap on the cellar door, but it made Hi Ling withdraw the knife, made the others turn their heads abruptly.

The Toff did not follow their example. He saw the roughneck step away from him and open the door, but he did not see the wizened ancient, although he heard his words.

'Mr. Ling—there is word for Mr. Ling.'

Chamberlain swore.

'Get to hell out of here before I—'

'A moment,' said Hi Ling. 'You forget that this is my house, mistah, these men my men. Yes, old one, what is it?'

'There's a 'phone message from the docks, Boss. The Customs is holding one o' the ships.'

Dougall swore.

'If it's—'

'Be silent!' snapped Hi Ling. He turned to Chamberlain, and at the same time glanced at the Toff, but expressionlessly. 'Mistah, I must go at once to see the reason for this delay. Dougall must also come. It will be well to keep Rollison here, unless—like me—you believe he will not talk, or knows nothing to talk of. Dead or alive he must stay here until I return.'

'Goddam you! Another ten minutes—'

'You have seen Rollison, yet you do not believe in him,' said Hi Ling. 'It cannot be helped, mistah; I must go, and go now. It may perhaps give you time to think, Rollison.'

He went out swiftly, with Dougall on his heels. Chamberlain swore for thirty seconds on end, then stopped himself and stood up from his chair.

'You can rot down here,' he snarled. 'Clear out, you!' He jerked a thumb towards the roughneck, who went out first. Rollison watched Chamberlain go, and heard the door close. A moment later the electric light, controlled by an outside switch, went out. The cellar was in complete darkness, and the only sound was the breathing of the two men.

At last Brendon muttered: 'It—it was ghastly, it—'

'Don't be a fool,' said the Toff equably. 'Worse things have happened and worse things will. I got off lightly, and while there's time there's hope. That was the trouble before.'

'There isn't a ghost of a chance, and—'

'There's a surprising lot of chances,' said the Toff, and he stopped rubbing his wrists to get the circulation back properly, and took a handkerchief from his trousers pocket. He tied it awkwardly about the top of his arm, so that it covered the burn and prevented chafing. 'Chamberlain has the wind up properly. He forgot I wasn't tied up.'

'How does that help?'

Both men were talking in whispers, as if to tone with the darkness and the silence. For a moment Rollison did not answer, but at last he said: 'I can free you, and there are chairs and boxes in here – while the door opens inwards. Oh, Chamberlain made a mistake all right; it's one of those chances that do come sometimes. Did you hear him talking of killing policemen?'

'No, I—*What?*'

'It is a point,' admitted Rollison. He could not see, but he reached Brendon by going in the direction of the man's voice, and he sought for the cords at the other's wrists. 'A knife would help, but we can't have everything, and they've rifled my pockets.'

'How the devil can you talk as if there was nothing the matter?' gasped Brendon.

'Can you tell me a better way to talk?' asked Rollison. 'If you want the whole truth, I'm so glad to be alive and whole for a few hours longer that I could sing many songs with great inaccuracy. Do you understand—that's one knot, rub your wrists while I do the ankle cords—that we've gained time, and the police will be after Chamberlain?'

'Why?'

'Because of the dead policemen,' said the Toff. 'I never hope to see a man who's absolutely scared stiff any more clearly than Chamberlain. He was desperate to hear whether I knew anything or not, whether I'd passed it on to the Yard, or … That's the other knot. Crawl about before you start walking.'

He was speaking for the sake of it, chiefly to get Brendon nearer to normal, although there was much truth and common sense in what he said. He did feel as though he had been under sentence of death, and had been reprieved, and the pain in his armpit was negligible.

His ears were alert for the slightest sound of approach, but none came. In ten minutes, Brendon was talking rationally, and able to walk fairly freely.

'All we need now is a light,' said the Toff.

His eyes were growing accustomed to the gloom, but as he walked about he stumbled against chairs and the table. But he collected them together near the door, and then went on his knees in the hope of finding a chopper or hammer that might prove useful as a weapon.

He found none.

He was hardly aware of the passing of time, but he began to feel hungry, and Brendon admitted he felt the same. Minutes dragged by, the waiting seemed interminable. There was no sound from above them, no hint of a return of Chamberlain and the others.

Rollison settled himself by the door, sitting with his back towards it, not daring to doze although the temptation was strong. It was maddening not to be able to tell the time while hearing the ticking of his watch clearly. He tried to estimate it, but beyond feeling sure that at least two hours had passed he could not do so.

At last he heard footsteps coming down the stairs.

The fact that Arnold Chamberlain was an alien helped in the speedy circulation of an accurate description. Little was said in the police radio that went out, but word of the two missing detectives was asked, as well as the detention of anyone answering Chamberlain's description. In that way nine men were detained in various parts of London, until each could prove his real identity.

At half past eleven McNab had nearly given up hope of quick results.

At twenty to twelve, while the harassed Chief Inspector was talking to the A.C. by telephone, a beat-policeman who had been off duty from eight o'clock – the call had gone out just after nine – was talking with a colleague on duty, and heard of the request for news about Chamberlain.

He said enough to make McNab hurry to the Bays-water Station, where the man would normally be stationed.

'This man ye saw,' said McNab brusquely. 'Can ye swear to him answering that description, Morgan?'

'Yes, sir, quite, sir. The man to a T, sir.'

'Where did you see him?'

'He got off a cab at Bayswater Road Station, sir, and walked down Queen's Road. It looked unusual, sir, getting out of a cab and then walking. I saw him go into Number 29a.'

'How is it you remember the number?'

'It's a boarding-house, sir; there's been some rum customers there at different times.'

As near as he could, McNab felt excitement.

'Right. Did you notice the number of the cab?'

'Sorry, sir, I didn't.'

'All right.' McNab lifted a telephone and sent a request for taxi-drivers who had deposited fares outside the station that evening to report to the Yard. He telephoned again for a Flying Squad car, for he was taking no chances. At ten past twelve he knocked heavily on the door of Number 29a, but there was no response. Three knocks were enough to convince McNab that either the house was empty or the occupier did not intend to open up. McNab, with the full authority of a search-warrant in his pocket, had one of his men force the door.

He found the place empty, until he reached the cellar. And after forcing the lock of the door he found Rollison and the youngster who had been at his flat – and both men were dirty and tired, but alive and well.

While the Toff admitted unreservedly that he had never been so overjoyed to see a policeman.

Later, when he was refreshed and bathed, and the burn in his armpit had been properly dressed, the Toff passed the opinion that Chamberlain and the others at the house had been warned of the police-call – rumours did get round, and Hi Ling would be one of the first to hear. Hi Ling, acting quickly and expertly, would have persuaded Chamberlain to leave the house, without harming

Rollison or Brendon. The Toff could almost hear the Chinaman telling Chamberlain that to commit more murder would be to ensure a rendezvous with the gallows.

'And he'd have been right,' said the Toff, leaning back in an easy chair, and, except for a more than usual paleness, looking none the worse for his adventure. 'For once I needed a hell of a lot of plain good fortune, my Mac, and you brought it to me.'

'Why didn't ye tell us all ye knew?' demanded McNab.

'I did. I know practically nothing, except ...'

The Toff gave a brief and not complete resume of what he did know, and McNab admitted that there was little he could have passed on to the police which was of useful purpose. It was not known at the time how accurate the Toff's estimate of Hi Ling's action and the departure of Chamberlain had been; later he knew that it had been almost word-perfect. For the moment: 'You'll want to have a go at Hi Ling's ships, Mac.'

'Ay. Rolleeson, did you see those two men of mine?'

'I did not.' The Toff looked, and felt, sombre. 'But I heard talk of killing policemen, Mac, and I'm afraid they've not had the same luck as I did.'

'Ach, no. Well, I'll be going. Ye need a good night's sleep, Rolleeson.'

'You're right, as always,' smiled the Toff,

He did not, however, propose to have a good night's sleep. He told a much-relieved Jolly that they were going down to Hersham, and he had little trouble in persuading Brendon to make the trip with him. In the small Frazer-Nash which Jolly drove the Toff alternately dozed and thought.

McNab now knew practically all he did – except the mention of the country house, and that, after all, was not knowledge but surmise – and the peculiar if small part Mr. Meer had played. That angle puzzled the Toff and he badly wanted to discover the possibilities behind it. It might, of course, mean nothing: on the other hand, an antique dealer in a sleepy old country town had wonderful opportunities for assisting in – for instance – drug distribution.

There was the Lowerby angle, too.

The Toff was, for once, inclined to wonder whether he should have made a clean breast of everything to McNab: certainly he owed the inspector that. On the other hand he was afraid that the many complications might result in the American slipping through the police net.

He did not expect Mannering to be pleased at being dragged from his bed at half past three in the morning, and he was right. But Mannering calmed down, told what little he knew of Mr. Meer, asked somewhat tentatively whether Rollison would be free for the next day's match – which was also the last of the cricket week – and was not surprised to learn that it was doubtful.

'What you can do for me,' said the Toff, 'is provide me with a bed, and then find me a register of empty houses in the neighbourhood that I can look at in the morning.'

'Empty what?'

'Houses,' said the Toff; and yawned so widely that Mannering asked no more questions. Twenty minutes after his arrival at the house the Toff was fast asleep, and in the servants' wing Jolly was also sleeping.

While through the darkness of the early hours Chamberlain, Hi Ling and Dougall sped from London towards Hersham.

Chapter Eighteen

Rough Stuff

The trio did not travel in the same car, but drove within half a mile of each other, all of them aware of the possibility that they would meet trouble before reaching the Sussex town. All of them had differing thoughts. Dougall was more frightened than anything else, and his hatred centralised on the Toff. Hi Ling was alarmed, but did not reveal that fact in his expression: he believed – in fact he knew – that Chamberlain's murder of the two C.I.D. officers had been the turning point of the affair.

The Chinaman knew that the flourishing coastal shipping business was smashed – the legal as well as the illegal side. The ship which had been held up by the Customs had contained, among other things, stolen jewels from Paris, and a fair-sized cache of cocaine. Once he had realised that, and known that the arrest of himself and Dougall was inevitable, he had gone to the 'Steam Packet', collected what available money he had there – and it was a substantial amount, for he had always prepared against emergency – and considered the situation.

Capital, even some thirty thousand pounds, would not last for ever. And Dougall was not so well off. There was need for quick action, and for quick money.

Had he followed his inclinations he would have neglected to warn Chamberlain when, through a runner at the 'Steam Packet', he had learned of the police call out for the American. But Chamberlain had money – not only as Chamberlain. He had more negotiable assets than Hi Ling or Dougall, and he had a hide-out near Hersham which might well prove a place of safety. There was no such harbour in London.

Hi Ling had warned Chamberlain, in consequence, of his knowledge.

There remained Hi Ling knew, the Sanderson angle, one that even now might yield considerable profit. Chamberlain had smashed a successful business in the trafficking in drugs and jewels, but he still had one hope of getting out with a handsome margin.

Part of which margin Hi Ling desired. Certainly amiable relations with Chamberlain were necessary, and Hi Ling remained amiable, after the arrangement to go in their separate cars to the Sussex hide-out.

Chamberlain – with his grey wig and the other items of disguise which made him less vulnerable to a police interrogation on the road than either of the others – was wondering how he could finish his work with the help of Hi Ling, and then avoid paying them for their services. He believed it could be done.

He swore to himself when he thought of the Toff. If the man had been made to talk …

Hi Ling should have made him. Hi Ling deserved all he got, but he was necessary for the time being. Necessary, in short, until such time as Chamberlain had all he wanted and could get out of the country. It might take two days, or even three; certainly neither Dougall nor Hi Ling were dangerous to him while he was at Hersham; he had one trick which they could not counter. They would try, he had no doubt: Hi Ling and Dougall were as suspicious of him as he of them.

But Chamberlain, calmer now that the first rush of danger from the police was past, had confidence in his greater efficiency.

And he laughed when he realised that Dr. Vincent Lowerby was going to get some shocks.

On the following morning the Toff awakened just after nine, feeling considerably refreshed even if his right armpit was somewhat more painful than he liked.

Jolly brought in the morning tea.

'It was through you, sir, that the police suspected Chamberlain of illegal operations,' he said. 'Through you that Dougall and Hi Ling were suspected of being concerned in this affair, and therefore through you that the Customs authorities held up the ship which prevented Hi Ling and Dougall from—er—completing their self-imposed task. Consequently, sir, you might be said to have been the leading figure in the arrival of the police at Queen's Road, and—'

'I know, I saved myself,' smiled the Toff. 'Your loyalty does you credit, but in any case it was just one of those things. Meanwhile, we're going to be busy. Is Mr. Brendon all right?'

'Yes, sir. I ran his bath for him twenty minutes ago. He appears in somewhat bad temper, sir.'

'In the circumstances we can't blame him. Did Sir George provide that register of empty houses?'

'Yes, sir, it is here.'

'Imagine a reasonably wealthy Australian who was going to buy a wedding present for his only daughter,' said the Toff, 'and pick out any houses you think might fit the bill.' He grinned as he gave the instructions, and went into the bathroom. When he returned, still more refreshed, he found Jolly at a table in his room, with a pencil in one hand, a mass of papers in front of him, and a close approach to a worried frown on his forehead.

'As bad as that, is it, Jolly?'

'I've selected every house over five thousand pounds,' said Jolly conservatively, 'and there are twenty-three of them within a twenty-mile radius of Hersham, sir.'

'Hmm.' The Toff began to dress, and his voice was somewhat muffled from beneath his shirt. 'Have you a map?'

'Yes, at my side, sir.'

'Have you marked the field where the body was found?'

'My pencil is on it, sir.'

'Take your pencil along the London road for a while,' said the Toff, 'and find all side-turnings that you can. Go, say, for ten miles, and then try to find the empty houses fairly near the main road on either side. Follow?'

'Yes, sir ...' Jolly carried on with his work. The Toff finished dressing. When he stepped to his man's side Jolly had the particulars of three houses separated from the others, and he handed them to the Toff.

'They would appear to be the most likely, sir. You will note that on the particulars of one the estate agents have marked: "Let for one year, but possession might be obtained for a serious buyer earlier." It is not, therefore, likely to be empty at the moment.'

'No-o. Which one is it?'

'Wyndham Manor, sir. The particulars, according to the list, suggest an extremely attractive Elizabethan property.'

'My acquaintance with house agents is limited,' said the Toff, 'but I'm told they're prone to exaggeration. Jolly, have a look at these three places—Wyndham Manor can be included as you're bound to pass nearby—and let me know what you think of them. You might take young Brendon with you since he's come. It will make him feel that he's being active.'

'I'll do that, sir.' Jolly collected the other papers and made a neat pile. 'Where are your movements likely to be?'

Rollison grinned.

'Worried about the possibility of another fiasco like yesterday's? I'll be in Hersham, near Lowerby's, and conceivably near Mr. Meer's antique shop. In fact if you haven't heard from me by two o'clock you can tell Sir George that both places need immediate investigation.'

'Thank you, sir,' said Jolly, with obvious satisfaction.

The Toff went down to a belated breakfast to find Mannering not much earlier, and several other hearty-cricketers prepared to pull his leg on the matter of his investigations. Looking at them, five men in all, and all healthy and wealthy, an idea flashed through his mind that he did not immediately voice.

By half past eleven he was in Hersham.

He drove slowly past Mr. Meer's shop, and he saw the venerable antique dealer standing in the doorway of his shop, and smiling benevolently at the passing world. Rollison went into the post office, almost opposite, and watched Mr. Meer for nearly five minutes.

He was very thoughtful as he came out of the shop and drove

towards Lowerby's house.

From Mannering he had learned that Meer had been in Hersham for some three years, although he had spent much of his time in the South of France, where he fondly imagined that he was improving his health. There was nothing physically wrong with the man, but he was convinced that he was delicate. His main characteristics, as far as Mannering knew them, were generosity towards the poor, absent-mindedness, lack of will power, and a love of gossip. He was certainly not commercially minded.

The Toff, partly in consequence of that summary, wondered whether Mr. Meer did go to the South of France, and if he did whether it was because he was careful of his health.

Meer disappeared from his mind as he neared the pleasantly situated house of Dr. Vincent Lowerby. The house was ideal for a retired man of moderate means, a smallish place built within the past ten years, but on old-fashioned lines, helped by a delightful background of trees and gorse-covered hillsides. The Toff could not properly understand, however, why a practising doctor should select a house some three miles from the town itself. The nearest neighbour was nearly half a mile away.

He soon learned why.

Lowerby obviously practised a measure of vivisection, judging from the pens with rabbits, mice and guinea-pigs which were set up in the back garden. Vivisection often meant noise that neighbours did not approve of, but was that the only reason?

Rollison shrugged as he walked from his car, which he left in the road, along the short gravel drive to the front door. He rang the bell, to be answered by a middle-aged light-lipped woman who did not receive him with any warmth.

'I'd like to see Dr. Lowerby at once, please.' Incisiveness was obviously to be the method with her.

'The surgery hours—'

'The matter is important and private,' said the Toff sharply. 'Tell him I have a message from Mr. Chamberlain.'

The woman sniffed, and went into a room leading from the hall. A moment later she reappeared, to ask him to go in. Rollison entered – and Lowerby, dressed in a white smock as he sat at a big desk, started up in alarm.

'Rollison, what—'

'Wait until the door's shut,' said the Toff. The woman went out, sniffing audibly, and Lowerby gulped twice, revealing a prominent Adam's apple. 'Well, Lowerby, the time for fooling is over. I've come for a showdown.'

'What—what are you talking about? I—'

'Don't be a fool,' said the Toff, and he did not look amiable. 'Chamberlain's wanted for murder and the police are searching the whole country for him. Not only the murder of the tramp, but other, more crazy ones.'

'I—I don't understand—'

'You understand all right,' snapped the Toff. 'You've got just a chance of coming clean, Lowerby, giving me the whole story of your association with Chamberlain. Oh, I know you distribute snow for him, I know you test the consignments he gets from abroad for strength, I know you dilute it when supplies aren't free ...'

He did not know.

But it was the obvious thing a doctor would do, and as he saw Lowerby's expression he knew that it had hit the truth. He felt an inward exhilaration as he stepped towards Lowerby.

'Not a nice thing for the police to learn, but better than being an accessory to murder. I —'

Lowerby was crouching back, half on his chair, half standing. He looked away from the Toff, his tongue darting along his lip, and he looked towards the window.

Rollison did not know what he saw.

But it was obvious from his expression that someone – something – was there. And in that moment the Toff moved as fast as he had ever done in his life. He reached Lowerby, gripped the man's right wrist and swung him round so that he was between the window and his visitor.

He heard a soft *zutt!* and he knew it was the noise of a silenced automatic.

He felt Lowerby's body sag, heard the gasp that sprang to the doctor's throat. He released the man and dropped to one knee behind the shelter of the desk, and as he went he saw Hi Ling outlined against the window, while two bullets hummed over his head.

Lowerby fell to the floor with a thud that shook the walls.

Hi Ling stepped swiftly to one side, but not swiftly enough, for the Toff fired from the end of the desk, and his bullet struck the Chinaman's gun-arm. It all happened in a few seconds, the crisis which the Toff had deliberately precipitated, and less than a second more passed as he moved across the room and grabbed at Hi Ling before the Chinaman had recovered from the wound in his arm.

Hi Ling struggled, his lips set tightly, his eyes showing a malevolence that spelt murder.

'Don't waste your time,' growled Rollison. 'I knew that a visit here, alone, to Lowerby would bring results, and McNab will love to see you. I—'

He heard a *crack!* from somewhere not far off.

It was a sound unmistakable to the Toff's ears – that of a rifle-shot. He knew in that moment that someone else was watching the house, and he flung himself to one side. But he need not have worried, for the bullet struck Hi Ling between the shoulder-blades and the Chinaman coughed sickeningly as he staggered forward.

Rollison stopped him from falling.

He was afraid of another shot, but none came as he lowered the wounded man to the ground. Hi Ling was coughing horribly, and there was a speckle of blood on his lips, but he was trying to speak. The Toff put his ear close to the twisted lips, but he heard only an incoherent muttering, and quite suddenly Hi Ling stopped moving.

Which meant that Hi Ling was dead.

With Lowerby.

Both men had been prevented from talking; neither man could ever give evidence.

Chamberlain was fighting a brutal battle to save himself, and Chamberlain was somewhere nearby.

The Toff stepped to a telephone, called the Hersham police and then put through a call to London, for in his mind there was an idea which he believed could and would finish Chamberlain completely.

Chapter Nineteen

Blow For Brendon

'It's all so damned silly,' snapped Frank Brendon, 'looking at a lot of empty houses in the hope of finding the one that Mr. Sanderson might have had in mind. Does Rollison expect him to have written his name on the front door?'

Jolly might have shown annoyance in different circumstances, but he restrained his feeling.

'Hardly, sir. But I have known Mr. Rollison for a long time, and he rarely fails to have an excellent motive for everything he does. And, after all, we have seen only two houses. The third is quite near—I imagine that is the gate.'

It was the gate leading to Wyndham Manor, the gate through which James and Sylvia Sanderson had passed nearly a week before. It was looking as friendly and inviting as it had done to the Sandersons, and the surrounding countryside was as beautiful in the warmth of the June sun, the trees and shrubs that bordered the long drive were green and restful to the eye.

They came in sight of the house itself.

'An excellent property,' said Jolly in an almost professional manner. 'I—'

'What's the matter with you?' demanded Brendon.

'It would appear to be empty,' said Jolly precisely, 'and the agents suggested that it was occupied, or at least let to a tenant on a short lease.'

'Then what's the use of coming?' Mr. Sanderson wouldn't be interested in an occupied house.'

'No-o,' said Jolly slowly. 'It is unusual, sir, and Mr. Rollison believes in investigating the unusual.' He pulled the car up outside the front entrance, and both men climbed out.

The windows were without curtains, and two panes of glass were broken. There was a vague air of dilapidation about it which told its own story – and Jolly wished that the Toff were with him instead of Brendon.

'I'll try the door, sir ...'

He did so, but it was locked. The windows were fastened and the broken panes were set too high to be of service. Jolly interested himself in the lock of the front door while Brendon went towards the rear of the house, smoking, his hands deep in his pockets and a scowl on his forehead. In his heart he believed Rollison was trying to help him, but all the time there was a heavy weight of fear – fear for Sylvia and Sanderson.

He was sure he had seen Jim the previous day – but if he had, if Sanderson had had free entry into 29a Queen's Road, then there was ample evidence that he was associated in Chamberlain's vicious game.

Not a pleasing thought.

More by habit than in hope, he tried the handle of the back door, and he stood back startled when it opened. He hesitated for a moment, looking behind him to find that Jolly was not in sight, and then scowled and pushed the door wider open. He went through, and as he entered a small scullery he fancied that he heard the sound of movement ahead of him.

'Anyone there?'

He did not know that he was experiencing just the same qualms as Sylvia had done six days before.

No answer came.

Brendon hesitated, and then pulled a second door wider open. It led to a kitchen, and on a deal-topped table was bread, butter, dirty crockery – and the smell of cigarette smoke. Brendon felt a flush of excitement course through his veins, and he turned to call Jolly.

He did not turn far.

For the third time in his life he saw Nigger Dougall. Nigger was just behind him, and he was not grinning. Brendon drew back, clenched his fists and prepared to rush at the giant, but he might as well have rushed at a brick wall. Dougall flung him back savagely, and then clouted the side of his head, making his ears ring, sending him off his balance. As he staggered the negro leapt at him again, and put one great hand over his mouth to prevent him shouting. Brendon retained consciousness for less than thirty seconds, for a vicious blow from a blackjack struck the back of his head.

Dougall stopped him falling and lifted him as easily as a normal man would have lifted a child. He kicked the door open with his foot, carried the unconscious youngster through the kitchen quarters and towards the stairs. As he began to mount the stairs, footsteps came from behind him.

He stopped, but Chamberlain's voice reassured him.

'All right, get him upstairs. I saw it.'

'Okay,' said Dougall. 'Where's Ling?'

'Watching Lowerby,' lied Chamberlain, who knew that Hi Ling was dead. He was carrying a rifle and he stood it in one corner. 'Did Brendon come alone?'

'I think so, Boss.'

'All right; but do more than think in future.' Chamberlain followed the negro up the stairs to an attic room, and outside a closed door Jaggers was sitting, opposite a little wizened man who might have been a brother of the fellow who had trapped Rollison at Queen's Road. They were playing cards, but gathered them up as the newcomers arrived.

'You got him?' Jaggers exclaimed.

'He was snooping around,' Dougall said. 'Open de door.'

The door opened, and from a camp-bed in one corner of the attic room a slight figure moved. Sylvia …

Sylvia stared at the negro, and bit her lips. She remembered with even greater vividness the horror of the moment, now nearly a week old, and she started to tremble. And then she saw Brendon.

'Frank!'

The single word seemed to break a spell which had been on her since the visit to the house. She forgot everything in a sudden fear for him, and as Dougall lowered the youngster not gently into a chair she flew towards him and went on her knees.

'Frank! Frank! …'

Dougall went out, and the door closed, the key turned in the lock. Chamberlain grinned.

'That's most of it, anyway. Brendon didn't know enough to make Rollison dangerous now. We'll get away with it, Dougall.'

'Sure, sure; but how long'll we be?'

'A couple of days,' said Chamberlain harshly. 'Don't you start getting worried about that. It's going to work out. This is one place Rollison won't find.'

'Brendon did,' snapped Dougall.

'Surely, I know, but—' Chamberlain broke off and hesitated. In the satisfaction of getting Brendon he had forgotten that Rollison might have sent the youngster here. He saw again that Dougall would present complications; Dougall knew a lot too much for his safety.

'That's okay,' he said. 'I can handle it all right, Dougall. You and Hi Ling won't have to worry. I'll be waiting on the next floor; you three can play cards. Don't forget I'm expecting a visitor, but I'll let him in. You three stay here.'

The men nodded, and Chamberlain went to a bedroom on the next floor, which was partly furnished. He stood by the window, looking over the drive. He was going through the affair as far as he could, recalling the long chain of circumstances that had started it. Nearly thirty years before, on an arid Australian plain, when he had committed murder …

Now he had the girl where she couldn't talk; Brendon – who might have been dangerous; and Sanderson, who was dead. Chamberlain chuckled, but his expression altered when he caught a glimpse of something moving along the drive. At first all he could see was the glitter of the sun on a polished surface, but after a few seconds he saw and recognised the small car coming to the house.

He hurried downstairs.

Two minutes later he opened the door to admit the man whom Brendon had seen on the previous day – a man who looked for all the world like James Sanderson, particularly from a distance. Brendon would have recognised a difference at close quarters, and so would Sylvia. But casual acquaintances, and James Sanderson had few others, would take it for granted that it was the Australian.

The man like Sanderson smiled.

'Howdy, Chamberlain. Things okay?'

'Working well,' said Chamberlain. 'We've got all the real danger over. I can scram in twenty-four hours and you can take over. I won't,' he added meaningly, 'be going far. Don't kid yourself about that.'

'Me and double-crossing don't go together.' The other man chuckled. 'You don't have to worry; you've got too much on me. Where's the Chink?'

'Where he can't talk, and the nigger's going that way soon. We'll have a clean-up upstairs before we go; put them all right out. Brendon is there, the girl, Jaggers and that little runt Ling gave us for a caretaker. We'll sit pretty, Matthews; it's okay by us.'

'That's dandy. Seen more of Rollison?'

Chamberlain grinned.

'He's around, but that's no worry. Lowerby's out, too; we've had a good clean-up.' The callousness of the words seemed natural, and the other man merely shrugged. 'We just stay here,' went on Chamberlain, 'until later in the day.'

Matthews rubbed his chin. His likeness to Sanderson was uncanny, but his manner was altogether different.

'I wish Rollison was looked after. Can't you work it?'

Chamberlain hesitated.

'There's maybe one way. Yes, one way. I'll try, Matthews—it's safe enough to try, anyway.'

'There is no doubt about it at all, sir,' said Jolly. 'Brendon completely disappeared, and a few minutes afterwards I saw Chamberlain enter the house. I had been fortunate enough to leave the car where he could not see it as he approached from the rear, and as soon as he was out of sight I coasted down the drive, which has a slight decline, and was able to start the engine out of sight and earshot of the house.'

'It's our spot,' said Rollison slowly. 'No doubt about it. And we need to move fast, Jolly. And if the gang's there, or what's left of it, we need men. In a hurry.'

'Yes, sir.'

Rollison said: 'Jolly, this game of cricket today is going to be interrupted. It's been started half an hour, and Mannering's in the field, but he'll come out. Telephone the police—Dawbury's the man you want—and tell him I'm sending the cricketers to Wyndham Manor, all armed with guns of some kind—Mannering has a gun-room full—with instructions to cover all possible exits. That means we won't be working unofficially. You might even say that it is Sir George's idea.'

'An excellent one, sir, if I may—'

'Get to the phone.' The Toff hurried towards the cricket field, seeing the white-flannelled figures moving slowly across at the end of an over, and he startled them with a cry that made every eye turn his way. Mannering glared.

'Sorry,' said Rollison. 'Gather round, folks—'

'Rollison, this is going too far!'

'And I've hardly started. George, half a dozen more or less of the tramp murderers, plus young Brendon, possibly plus the girl, are at Wyndham Manor. Suggest that you put a shotgun or a rifle into each man's hand and fling a cordon round the place. No one to go in or out. I've told Dawbury,' he added cheerfully, 'that it was your idea.'

'Good Gad!' gasped Mannering. 'I—Rollison, it's a stroke of genius! I—' He turned sharply to the others. 'This might be dangerous, but all who will help …'

A moment later twenty-two white-clad men hurried towards the gun-room at the Ridings, with Mannering at their head. Rollison was with him as far as the door, and then said: 'No one in, no one out, old man. I'll be along soon.'

'What? Aren't *you* coming?'

'No; I want to talk with Mr. Meer,' said the Toff. And he lifted a hand and hurried away.

Chapter Twenty

Of Mr. Meer

Mr. Augustus Meer had been out most of the morning, but when the bell at his shop door rang he was in the gloomy recesses and apparently working on some figures. He hurried forward, paused when he saw a tall man enter the shop, and spoke affably.

'Good morning, sir. Is there anything I can do for you?'

Rollison smiled as only he could.

'I've seen a most interesting piece of Burmese filigree work in your window, and I wondered—'

'Ah—*Burmese* filigree,' said Mr. Meer, and he launched a long discourse on filigree, Burmese and other wise, which lasted for ten minutes. Rollison evinced no impatience although he inserted a question now and again to show that his interest was intelligent. Finally: 'The piece in the window,' Mr. Meer went on, 'is hardly *first* class, sir, but I have—I would not say this to anyone who was not obviously an expert—some excellent examples in my study upstairs, if you would care to inspect them. I would offer to bring them down but—'

'I'll come up with pleasure,' said Rollison.

In the gloom the glint in Meer's eyes was not obvious, and he turned and led the way up a flight of narrow, twisting stairs. Rollison followed carefully, and entered a room which was as gloomy as most of the shop, for the curtains were drawn across small windows, allowing only a filter of light to get through. Unlike the shop, however, the room was in excellent order, and about it were several genuine examples of Sheraton, Chippendale' and Louis-Seize pieces. On one wall was a small collection of Burmese filigree, marvellously executed, some of it probably the labour of years.

'You see,' said Mr. Meer eagerly. 'If you care to examine them more closely, I will switch on. the light.'

He switched it on while the Toff pored over the pieces in his hands. By the door Meer hesitated, as if uncertain, and then in a slightly higher voice than usual he said: 'Oh, excuse me …'

The Toff turned, and he looked at the automatic in Meer's hand. It might have been a repetition of what had happened at Queen's Road, except for one thing – of which Meer was not aware.

Rollison stared.

'My dear sir, how absurd of you to try to come here on business,' chuckled Mr. Meer. 'If you suspected my interest in the affairs of Chamberlain, surely you realised I would be well acquainted with your appearance. A grave mistake, a very grave mistake.'

Rollison looked stupefied.

'I—Good Lord, this—'

'Don't, please, try to bluff,' said Meer testily. 'It means wasting so much time, and we don't want that. Do you know, Mr. Rollison, I think you and I will take a little journey. To join poor young Brendon and that unhappy girl.'

Rollison said slowly: 'So you know where she is? Did you help to kill her father?'

Meer started.

'But—' He broke off and chuckled. 'You were not convinced then that Brendon saw James Sanderson? Well, it can do little harm now, you may know that he didn't. A man most amazingly like Sanderson, and—'

Rollison said slowly: 'I wondered if that was the game, Meer. Sanderson disappears, his hands are mutilated to make positive identification impossible. But you don't mind a tramp being found – the tramp was needed just to provide a body. Meaning,' he added gently, while Meer continued to stare and continued to threaten with his automatic, 'that the body of the tramp was nicely disposed of so that Sanderson's body could be got rid of more conveniently. The one important thing was that no one should suspect that Sanderson was dead.'

'You—you amaze me,' said Meer. 'I'm sure Chamberlain had no idea of the accuracy of your deductions.'

'You ought to know,' said the Toff, and he eased his shoulders back, as if to dispose of a dead weight. 'You kept the girl because you knew Brendon would come after her, and if necessary she would have sent some word showing Brendon she was alive, bringing him into your blasted trap. Only Brendon and Sylvia could have identified James Sanderson definitely in this country—.'

'In all countries, I hope,' said Mr. Meer gently.

'Maybe you hoped rightly,' said the Toff, and he eased his shoulders back again. 'Your man—the man Brendon saw—was to take Sanderson's place, and take control of his business and his money. Nicely arranged, Meer.'

'Yes, wasn't it? I don't mind admitting that it was *my* idea. You make one mistake, however. You say "was" and you mean "is". Both Brendon and the girl are in our hands, and you—I'm afraid this time you will not get away, Mr. Rollison, and after all you can hardly expect your luck to last for ever.'

'No-o,' said Rollison. He looked at the gun, and then into Meer's weak eyes, hidden so well by his thick-lensed glasses. 'I suppose not. You—er—your men killed Sanderson, then the tramp. Sanderson's real body was identified as the tramp's, and the tramp's will never be identified at all, certainly not as Sanderson. Oh, it was neat, Meer. But you had rather too many complications.'

'I'll admit that,' said Meer handsomely.

'Yes. You ran drugs and you ran a big fence's business, you cut stolen stones here and sent them to Chamberlain's office through Lowerby—who thought he was putting one over on you and Chamberlain. Lowerby was in it for his work on the drugs, of course; Hi Ling and Dougall merely provided your working arrangements, plus a useful share in the snow and the jewels. Quite a big business was built up—and Mr. Chamberlain, in and out of the country as he has been, has been the prime mover all the time.

That's right?'

'Yes, yes; but really you—'

'A moment,' said Rollison evenly. 'There isn't a lot more to be explained, but Chamberlain killed two policemen. You know that, of course.'

'Yes, a mistake, almost an accident, but ...' Meer shrugged. 'Step this way, Mr. Rollison, please. And although I would much rather you had a talk with Chamberlain first, don't make any foolish move or I shall be compelled to shoot you here and now. Most disturbing, and—'

'A pity to bring the police here,' Rollison said. 'You wouldn't like that at all.' He stepped towards the door and Meer kept a safe distance, with the gun trained on him all the time. 'Not at all, my friend. I told you once before that you were a good actor, didn't I? A poor crook but a good actor.'

Meer stared; and then he swore. His voice was no longer mild and benevolent, it was harsh and overbearing – *Chamberlain's voice!* Chamberlain!

'Goddam you, you knew—'

'Oh, yes,' said the Toff evenly, 'I knew when I saw you this morning: your grey wig makes you very much like you were on the night at the "Steam Packet". That's the trouble with crooks, Chamberlain, they always overlook something, and you overlooked that. As Mr. Meer you had a completely separate identity; you could have lived in England—or gone to France—without the slightest fear from the police. *If* it had worked out your way.'

'It'll work out!' snarled Arnold Chamberlain. 'I—'

'Look just behind you,' said the Toff, 'and meet Chief-Inspector McNab, of Scotland Yard. An interested listener, who came down in response to a phone call this morning.'

'Don't try tricks! I—'

And then a heavy hand descended on Meer's gun-arm, the gun was wrenched away, while burly Inspector McNab said, without humour: 'But it isn't a trick. Thanks, Rolleeson.'

'No one in, and no one out,' said the Toff easily, 'Nice work, George, but we're in something of a spot. We want to get in now.'

'We've got to get them out first,' said Mannering. 'I know there's someone there, we've seen them at the windows. The Nigger, for one. What the deuce did you go off to see that man Meer for?'

'I wanted to get to know him better,' said the Toff. 'We can talk later, old man, but first we've got to move. Have your people been seen?'

'I don't think so; they've kept well out of sight behind the trees and bushes. Rollison, I wish you'd explain a little more.'

'All the explaining needed for the moment,' said the Toff, 'is that two prisoners and three murderers are at Wyndham Manor. If we make a rush, the prisoners aren't likely to have a good time, and one of them's a girl. I think—Is Jolly about?'

'Here, sir,' said Jolly from nearby. They were near the drive and they could see a part of the house through the trees.

'We'll do it,' said Rollison, 'We'll drive up as if we're on our own. Get the door open and then our flannelled fools and what police have arrived can rush. I shall need five minutes inside to look after the girl.'

Mannering's red face was set in alarm.

'Are you serious? Do you know what you're risking?'

'I've had so much luck this time,' said the Toff, 'that a little risk will only be repayment. Let's get back to the car, Jolly. George, on your life, don't let a man move forward until we've been inside for five minutes. All right?'

'Ye-es ...' Mannering seemed dubious; but McNab, who arrived immediately on the Toff's words, assured him that it was the kind of thing Rollison was likely to do; while the Toff asked, reasonably, what other thing they could try.

For there was no hope for Brendon and the girl in a large-scale attack.

In three minutes Rollison's Frazer-Nash was running along the drive, with Jolly at the wheel and the Toff next to him, and looking about him, to the credit of the cricketers, he saw only an occasional patch of white, and when he climbed out of the car and looked from the house, he saw none.

'Well, Jolly?' he said.

'We need the luck, sir.'

'Right again. Well, bang on the door.'

The echoes of the knocking reverberated through the barely furnished house, and there was a minute of silence. As they waited Rollison saw the possibility of death, and the possibility was not remote. The men inside would be desperate, and without Chamberlain they lacked a leader. The one way to trick them was to make them believe Rollison and Jolly were not accompanied by the police.

Footsteps dragged along the floor.

Rollison put a hand to his pocket, and Jolly did likewise. The footsteps drew nearer – but before the door opened a voice snapped from behind them: 'Keep right ther'!'

It was Jaggers – and Jaggers with a gun. He had come from the back, taking no chances; and in the Toff's eyes there was an expression that suggested he had not dreamed of any attack.

Jaggers grinned, and his squint did not look less villainous.

'The Boss'll be glad to see yer! Okay, Nig, watch 'em.'

Dougall had opened the door, and in his hand, too, there was a gun. There was obvious reason for the Toff to try nothing, and he stepped over the threshold with Jolly in his wake. He knew that if any of the cordon about the house were seen it was his death-warrant, and Jolly's. But both Jaggers and Dougall seemed too relieved to have suspicions.

'And I thought you was smart,' grinned Dougall. 'Yessah, folks said you were smart. Pick yo' feet up them stairs.'

'You're making another mistake,' said Rollison, for it was the kind of thing he might be expected to say. For answer he had a clout on the side of the head from Dougall's vast hand, and he walked upstairs without speaking again. The old man was near the door of the attic room, and from the second landing a man hurried – Matthews – who was so like Sanderson.'

'My God—Rollison!'

'Sure t'ing! Easy meat!' grinned Dougall. 'De boss, he said he could do it; I guess he's plenty clever. Open de door, old man, and

…'

The ancient, first cousin to the man of Queen's Road, judging from appearances, opened the door. Rollison was pushed through roughly; Jolly was helped by a kick from the rear that offended more than hurt him.

'De boss will be back soon,' grinned Dougall. 'Take de fellas' guns, Jag, take dem.'

Jaggers unarmed the Toff and Jolly, while Brendon – conscious again – and Sylvia Sanderson stared at the new-comers. Brendon drew a sharp breath, and: 'So they got you too! We're finished. I—'

'You shut yo' trap,' grinned Dougall. 'Yo' finished okay.'

He went out and banged the door, and they heard the key turn in it. Brendon was pale-faced, the girl seemed to stagger on her feet, but to them both the Toff turned a beaming smile and for once the dyspeptic face of Jolly did its best to imitate the beam.

'It's precisely what the doctor ordered,' said the Toff. 'For once there's a climax when I just look on, and that's a pleasant change. Pull yourself together, Brendon. Give me a hand with getting all the furniture against the door.'

'But—'

'The police and others,' said Rollison, 'are about to raid the place, and this will be the safest spot by a long way.'

It was.

From the attic window, and taking it in turns to look out since they needed a chair to reach it, they watched the slow approach of the police, and they heard the shooting. Twice there were efforts to get into the attic room, but the door stood the strain while the ring of police – with the cricketers in support – came remorselessly closer. And then from the window the Toff saw Dougall and the man Matthews start to run, knew they had been forced out, and were taking a desperate chance.

Both men crashed down, wounded in the legs, before they had moved twenty yards. While inside Jaggers and the ancient were wounded and unable to offer any resistance when the police broke in.

The Toff smiled down on Sylvia and young Brendon. 'A bad break,' he said, 'but it's your innings now. I've told you most of what I learned from Meer, and all that I managed to piece together. We've been lucky, and that means you as well as me in many ways. It could have been a great deal worse.'

Brendon nodded.

'Of course, but—'

'You're going to ask why it started,' said the Toff. 'Well, it started in nineteen hundred and ten, when Jim Sanderson and Arnold Chamberlain lost a race for a gold-claim, and Chamberlain did murder. Both men were equally guilty in the eyes of the law, but whereas Chamberlain kept crooked, Sanderson went straight. He did well, but Chamberlain kept demanding payment for silence—and since your father, Miss Sanderson, did not know where Chamberlain was and could not answer threat by threat, he paid. That's why he was always worried, why he kept himself to himself—he was always afraid.'

The girl nodded, and if her face was pale she showed no signs of breaking down.

'Chamberlain grew more insistent with his demands, and your father decided to retire and come to England. Chamberlain suspected such a move, and sent Jaggers to Australia to watch all developments. Consequently he knew just when you left Australia and—as Chamberlain, a different name from that he had used when your father knew him—he struck an acquaintance, sold you a fur cape, talked of flats and houses, and generally behaved as a friend. He was doing very well, but he was tired of keeping windward of the law, and after he saw your father he knew that he had this man Matthews to use for—well, call it stepping into your father's shoes.'

'The beastly swine!' said Brendon gruffly.

'Nothing stronger than that?' asked the Toff. 'Sanderson—the false Sanderson—had to be trained to take your father's place: it couldn't be done in too much hurry. It looked fool-proof, too, except that they made a mistake in letting you see he was actually murdered. However—it was just that shade too complicated; Chamberlain had one iron too many in the fire.'

'It's as well he did,' said Sylvia quietly. 'I don't know how to thank you, Mr. Rollison.'

'Thank me?' said the Toff in surprise. 'It's me to thank you; I enjoyed it. Particularly the last act. I've never felt so safe and comfortable in my life. Well ...'

It was a week after the raid on Wyndham Manor when the two youngsters left his flat, after shaking hands warmly, a moment when Sylvia had been very close to tears. The Toff watched them walking along Gresham Terrace with Jolly at his side.

'A nice couple, Jolly.'

'Yes, sir. And a nice haul, if I may say so.'

'Yes. But let it be a lesson to you. Jolly; don't go in for too many complications when you turn to a life of crime. Well—McNab's happy, and Dawbury's happy, and we're happy and Sir George Mannering is certainly well content, so—'

'I beg leave to differ, sir,' said Jolly dispassionately. 'Sir George was on the telephone this afternoon, sir. He is arranging another cricket week, in view of the fact that the last one was so disturbed, and he is hoping you will be available for *every* match, sir.'

The Toff grinned.

'I take my hat off to him, Jolly,' he said. 'Certainly we will go.'

John Creasey

Gideon's Day

Gideon's day is a busy one. He balances family commitments with solving a series of seemingly unrelated crimes from which a plot nonetheless evolves and a mystery is solved.

One of the most senior officers within Scotland Yard, George Gideon's crime solving abilities are in the finest traditions of London's world famous police headquarters. His analytical brain and sense of fairness is respected by colleagues and villains alike.

'The finest of all Scotland Yard series' – New York Times.

Gideon's Fire

Commander George Gideon of Scotland Yard has to deal successively with news of a mass murderer, a depraved maniac, and the deaths of a family in an arson attack on an old building south of the river. This leaves little time for the crisis developing at home ....

'Gideon of Scotland Yard emerges as one of the most real working detectives in modern fiction.... A sympathetic and believable professional policeman.' - New York Times

JOHN CREASEY

THE CREEPERS

"The prisoner's hand was thin and bony ... And in the centre of the palm was a pinkish mark. It was the shape of a wolf's head, mouth open, fangs showing. Although it was what he had expected to see, Inspector West felt a twinge of repugnance a stab not unrelated to fear. It was the fifth time he had seen the mark of the wolf – the mark of Lobo."

A gang of cat burglars led by Lobo cause mayhem as they terrorize the city. They must be stopped, but with little in the way of evidence the police are baffled. Just how can Inspector West manage to do this in what is a race against time before more victims succumb?

"Here is an excellent novel of law enforcement officers, harried, discouraged and desperately fatigued, moving inexorably ahead under the pressure of knowledge that they must succeed to save human lives." - Cleveland Plain-Dealer

"Furiously exciting" - Chicago Tribune

"The action is fast, continuous and exciting" - San Francisco News

John Creasey

Introducing the Toff

Whilst returning home from a cricket match at his father's country home, the Honourable Richard Rollison - alias The Toff - comes across an accident which proves to be a mystery. As he delves deeper into the matter with his usual perseverance and thoroughness , murder and suspense form the backdrop to a fast moving and exciting adventure.

'The Toff has been promoted to a place of honour among amateur detectives.' – The Times Literary Supplement

Case Against Paul Raeburn

Chief Inspector Roger West has been watching and waiting for over two years – he is determined to catch Paul Raeburn out. The millionaire racketeer may have made a mistake, following the killing of a small time crook.

Can the ace detective triumph over the evil Raeburn in what are very difficult circumstances? This cannot be assumed as not eveything, it would seem, is as simple as it first appears .....

'Creasey can drive a narrative along like nobody's business ... ingenious plot ... interesting background .' - The Sunday Times

14477817R00097

Printed in Great Britain
by Amazon.co.uk, Ltd.,
Marston Gate.